'Sleep well.'

It reached her only as a murmur. Looking back just before she rounded the corner of the bridge, Jennie saw that he had already turned to stare out to sea again. Funny. . . What he had told her tonight about his past career ought to have left her feeling that she knew more about the man. In fact it was the opposite. Did Dr Gray know just what a dark horse he seemed?

Dear Reader

We're only travelling far with one book this month, as Lilian Darcy takes us cruising Bermudan waters in RUNNING AWAY. A MAN OF HONOUR by Caroline Anderson is a deeply moving book, while Jean Evans gives us her first vet book set on Jersey with THE FRAGILE HEART. Elizabeth Harrison gives us a hero with spinal injuries in THE SENIOR PARTNER'S DAUGHTER, all of which makes up a perfectly super month. Do enjoy!

The Editor

Lilian Darcy is Australian, but on her marriage made her home in America. She writes for theatre, film and television, as well as romantic fiction, and she likes winter sports, music, travel and the study of languages. Hospital volunteer work and friends in the medical profession provide the research background for her novels; she enjoys being able to create realistic modern stories, believable characters, and a romance that will stand the test of time.

Recent titles by the same author:

NO MORE SECRETS
HEART CALL

RUNNING AWAY

BY
LILIAN DARCY

MILLS & BOON LIMITED
ETON HOUSE, 18–24 PARADISE ROAD
RICHMOND, SURREY, TW9 1SR

*First published in Great Britain 1994
by Mills & Boon Limited*

© Lilian Darcy 1994

*Australian copyright 1994   Philippine copyright 1994
This edition 1994*

ISBN 0 263 78591 2

*Set in 10 on 11 pt Linotron Times
03-9405-57047*

*Typeset in Great Britain by Centracet, Cambridge
Made and printed in Great Britain*

CHAPTER ONE

'AND so. . . Why did you take this job, hmm?' asked Dr Hector Mendez, lounging back in the yellow taxi and studying Sister Genevieve McDougall with his wide, light green eyes.

Jennie stiffened. Just the question she *didn't* want to face when she was disorientated following her transatlantic flight and more disorientated at the sight of the New York city-scape that was unfolding all around her.

Suppressing a red-headed impulse to snap at him, None of your business, Dr Mendez! in her expressive Scottish border-country accent, she manufactured a smile that made creamy eyelids crease around summer-blue eyes and said mildly, 'Oh, the same reason as anybody, I suppose. I wanted to travel.'

Dr Mendez nodded intently and said with an extravagant sweep of the hand, 'Yes! To see all this! It makes one humble. Me, I sometimes wonder if I will ever return to Colombia. To be privileged by our profession to see all this!'

'Well—er——' Jennie glanced out of the window. At this particular moment they were stuck in traffic, jammed in with a handful of exhaust-snorting trucks and half a dozen honking taxis in a pothole-filled street. The only vistas offered were vertical ones, up, up to where a swath of chilly grey April sky seemed to be fighting a losing battle against buildings that towered ever taller above the littered pavements.

She was about to comment that this wasn't *quite* the panorama she had dreamed of when she had answered an advertisement seeking an experienced nurse at short

notice for work on a luxury cruise ship. In fact, for
some reason, she had been thinking more of *oceans*. . .
But then she saw that Hector Mendez was quite serious.

She said instead, 'Yes, to be able to travel with one's
work is a privilege, I suppose.'

The taxi moved on and its two passengers were silent
for several minutes. Jennie used the time to study her
companion. He was not a tall man, but she knew that
many women would consider him good-looking. A
Colombian father and a German mother — he had given
her a brief autobiography as their taxi drove through
Brooklyn — had given him the unusual combination of
golden-tanned skin, light brown hair and green eyes
coupled with an exotically handsome bone-structure.

It had been a relief to find him at the airport waiting
for her, as she had not known whether to expect
anyone, and had wondered if she would correctly
interpret the instructions she had been given about how
to make her way from Kennedy International Airport
to the cruise ship terminal on the Hudson river. After a
flight which she had spent largely in unproductive inner
questioning about whether this new job was just running away, the warm arm he had placed around her
shoulders as he greeted her had been pleasantly
reassuring.

Impulsively she said now, 'Thank you for coming to
meet my flight. It really made a lot of difference.'

He gave a Latin shrug. 'Of course I had to meet you!
How could I let a woman cross the city alone after a
tiring flight? I said to myself, She will be homesick,
tired. I have little else to do with my hours off, and I
received permission to come.'

'Well, it was a real relief. Thank you for giving up
your time off.'

'This is your first time in New York, I think.'

'Yes.'

'Perhaps your first time out of England. . .'

'No, I've been out of England before.' Once. Last Christmas. With Ralph. They had spent a week in Spain, and she *didn't* want to think about that, or about Ralph Caine at all. She went on quickly, 'And what about you? Are you well travelled?'

He shrugged again. 'Before this job I had barely left Colombia. But for me, you see, it is not the places, it is the people. To meet a woman, for example, on her holidays, alone, carefree. To make a connection with her, and to say goodbye, knowing we have enriched each other's lives.' He gave a smouldering, sensuous smile.

'Oh,' said Jennie, startled into a characteristic frankness that she didn't always remember to control. 'I see. That's the reason you like this job! The female passengers!'

He laughed, unrepentant. 'I'm a very physical man. I like to touch and to be touched.'

He leaned a little closer to her as he spoke and Jennie leaned exactly the same distance away, saying very firmly, 'Do you? Well, I don't! And if you think that's why I'm here, then you've got another think coming.'

He was lazily amused. 'You British! Anthony is just the same. Dr Gray. You will meet him soon. As a nation, you are made of wood, it seems. The stiff upper lip, is that the expression? Won't you learn to bend a little in the tropical heat, Jennie? Let the sun soften your limbs so that they want to reach out to a man and——'

'No!' It was a sharp, angry syllable. She didn't intend to explain to Hector Mendez that frigidity in affairs of the heart was *not* her problem. In fact, she didn't intend to explain to anybody. She had taken this job precisely to escape from too much probing and questioning from friends, colleagues and family. She needed to heal

herself after Ralph's double betrayal and her conse-
quent loss of confidence, yes, but she needed to do it
alone.

This time, after her too-abrupt response, Hector's
laugh was a little awkward, although he turned it into a
joke against her by pretending to cower back in the
corner of the taxi. 'Please! If I have hit a raw nerve. . .'

Jennie didn't answer at all for a moment, then the
taxi turned a corner and she saw the ship, its bows
rising above the dock in a gracefully curved wall of
white. 'That's it, isn't it?' she said excitedly. 'That's the
Leeward.'

'Yes, isn't she magnificent?' Hector answered with a
possessive caress in his tone, and for the moment
awkwardness was forgotten.

In a few hours that ship would be leaving harbour, to
slip south-east through Atlantic seas until it gradually
left the bleak seascapes of a late spring to enter the
aquamarine waters of the Gulf Stream. Surely then,
very quickly, she would forget Ralph and the stinging
blow he had delivered to her professional confidence
and her personal sense of worth.

Dr Mendez paid off the taxi, took Jennie's two
suitcases and nudged her ahead of him, pointing the
way to the crew's special entrance and customs check-
in. It was almost noon and passengers were not yet
boarding, so that the echoing hall that ran the length of
the wharf parallel to the ship was nearly empty. One or
two crew members came and went as Jennie's papers
were checked. There were two small dark officers
speaking Greek, a lone man who looked to be Filipino,
perhaps, and a crisply uniformed American woman
with a male companion who looked American, too.

'Our crew is made up of thirty-seven nationalities,'
Hector told her.

And then they were aboard, treading on soft carpeting as they entered a glittering golden lobby. 'It's like a hotel, not a ship!' Jennie exclaimed as they went down a spiralling sweep of gold-railed stairs and started along a silent corridor of astonishing length.

'The *Leeward* is only three years old. It is what Americans expect now when they cruise. No more indoor steel gangways and cabins the size of a small bath-tub. You should see the luxury cabins on Deck Nine.'

'I doubt I will,' Jennie returned mildly. 'But I expect you have!' He laughed, utterly unabashed at the innuendo. Well, I've already found out how to deal with him, Jennie thought. I wonder what Dr Gray will be like. . .?

She found out soon enough. Hector handed her a flat grey plastic card with a pattern of holes punched into it and said, 'Your key. It looks more like a credit card, I know.'

'How do I —— ?'

He took it back from her after she had fumbled with it in the door's metal slit, pushed it neatly in and pulled a handle. The door opened with a click. 'You will soon get the idea,' he told her. 'You share with Tilly Balasingham. She must be still ashore.'

Jennie saw an emerald blouse hanging over a chair and a paperback novel on the small night-table that separated the twin beds. Above each bed were small sets of cupboards and there was just room enough between the end of the unoccupied bed and the cabinet bathroom for suitcases to be stored. With her personal belongings here as well as Sister Balasingham's, it would get cramped, but perhaps neither of the nurses would be spending a lot of time here.

'Don't unpack now, if you don't mind,' Hector said. 'Dr Gray wants to see you straight away.'

Thus, with scarcely a chance to acquaint herself with

what would be home for the next six months—and longer if she decided at the end of that time to renew her contract on the *Leeward*—Jennie found herself following in Hector's wake once again, back towards the magnificent stairwell and lift bay.

This time there was no need to go up or down a deck. Just along from the lifts, a bland beige door opened into the ship's hospital, where a small waiting-room gave on to several closed doors and an open corridor. Hector Mendez knocked at the door marked 'Surgery' and a crisp, deep male voice—very English—called, 'Come in.'

Hector made a face that seemed to say, See, such a typical Britisher! Even his tone is stiff, then he opened the door to usher Jennie in to meet the ship's senior physician.

It was strangely unnerving to meet a fellow country-man here in this new world. Anthony Gray stood up behind the desk at which he had been sitting and leaned forward to shake her hand. It was a cool, brief touch, conveying little about the senior doctor, who looked to be aproaching his middle thirties. The man's name suited him, Jennie decided at once. In fact, it suited him rather too well. He *looked* grey, his face tired and tense so that the pallor of his skin drew the colour away from what would otherwise have been very striking eyes. Grey eyes. Dark, slatey ones fringed by sooty lashes. They burned in his face today beneath a tight frown, and she wondered what was wrong. . .

'You might as well go, Hector. Grab a couple of hours off before we sail,' the Englishman said in a controlled tone. 'Thanks for meeting Sister McDougall.' A moment later, they were alone, with the door closed discreetly by the junior physician, and Dr Gray went on, 'I'm sorry I couldn't be there myself. I fully intended to, but we had an ill passenger who

needed a transfer to hospital and that always involves
phone calls and paperwork. Hector was gracious about
it, I hope?'

'Oh, very!' In fact, the junior medical officer had
given Jennie the distinct impression that coming to
meet her flight had been exclusively his own idea.

The smooth deception, reflecting well on himself,
didn't surprise Jennie, as she felt that she had already
taken the man's measure and would continue to take
him, from now on, with a generous pinch of salt.
Having now reached the age of twenty-six, she had
considered herself a good judge of people until
recently, and then she had been so terribly, painfully
wrong about Ralph. To find that Hector was behaving
in character, as she had assessed him, was a first, tiny
step in her healing. Recognising this, Jennie let a small
smile break on to her face, very glad for the moment
that she *had* taken the step of throwing up her job at
Newcastle's Edgewater Grange Hospital — Ralph's hospital — to come here to the *Leeward*.

Then she saw that Anthony Gray's frown had deep-
ened as he studied her, and realised that she had to
concentrate on this interview with her new senior.

'You enjoyed your flight?' he was asking
perfunctorily.

'Yes. I was a wee bit nervous, of course.'

'Nervous?'

'It's a big change to make at two weeks' notice.' She
realised too late that she had opened the way for
another unwanted question about her motives in leaving England, but Anthony Gray ignored the
opportunity.

'You'll settle in,' he said. 'I hope you don't get
seasick.'

'So do I! I expect I'll find out soon enough.'

She expected at least a polite smile at this, but Dr

Gray's face remained very firmly set. He was fiddling with a pale pink sheet of paper that lay on the desk and Jennie saw now that it was a letter, lying face down on top of an envelope with an English stamp, so that only what was written on the back of the flimsy paper could be seen.

She caught sight of the words 'Best love, Mummy' written in mauve ink in a very flowery hand, then Anthony Gray followed the direction of her gaze, took the letter up and folded it roughly before stuffing it into a desk drawer.

'Post from home. That's nice,' Jennie said inanely.

'Yes.' But she got the strong impression that this particular letter, at least, had not given Anthony Gray any pleasure at all.

It was incongruous, too, to think that a woman writing to a man as impressive as this would still be signing herself as 'Mummy'. From his manner now, Jennie very much doubted that Dr Gray replied in the same vein. But. . .'impressive'? The word had come immediately to mind and fallen into place in her thoughts as if it fitted perfectly.

It did fit, too, she decided. Anthony Gray had risen from his seat now and was turning to take a manila folder off the shelf behind him. He was quite tall, yet wore very gracefully the white uniform of a ship's officer — neat, immaculately clean trousers and a short-sleeved shirt with black and gold epaulettes that indicated his rank. His hands were strong, with the lean yet powerful, delicate yet steely fingers of a surgeon. His arms were tanned and his face was, too, she realised. It hadn't seemed that way at first because he had looked so strained and washed out.

In fact, he still did. As he sat down and handed her the folder, he put a hand to his temple and pressed it hard, staying quite still for a moment. He was waiting for a spasm of pain to pass, she suddenly understood.

'You have a terrible headache, Doctor. Why don't you let me get you something for it?'

'No, thanks,' he said, through clenched teeth. Then he rose abruptly and lunged for the sink several feet away. 'Go into the waiting-room,' he ground out, and, understanding that he was about to vomit and wanted to do it alone, Jennie quickly left the surgery, shutting the door behind her.

She moved to the far end of the waiting-room to study some medical posters pinned to the walls and was only faintly able to hear the sound of running tap-water as Anthony Gray bent over the sink. It was several minutes before the surgery door opened again. Turning quickly, Jennie saw that Dr Gray was even paler than before.

'You look terrible,' she told him frankly. 'You should be lying down. You *must* take something. We're sailing in three hours, aren't we?'

'I don't need anything,' he answered fuzzily. 'I'll feel better in a few minutes. I always do after —— ' He broke off, then went on, 'What I'd like to do is to go up on deck for a while to get some air. Will you come? I'm sorry about this. You must have questions and I want to be able to answer them, but I find it rather airless down here.'

'Of course I'll come,' she told him gently. 'I'd love to see the upper decks.'

'The passengers will be boarding by now and there's a buffet served on Deck Eleven.' He paused to sip some water from a glass, taking the liquid carefully through firm lips that were slightly fuller on top than on the bottom. 'We don't often eat with passengers, but you've missed lunch in the officers' mess. . .'

'And you've lost yours!'

'Actually I didn't get a chance to eat at all.'

'Well, no wonder you got a headache, then,' she chastised him gently.

For the first time, he gave a brief laugh, although he still held his face carefully immobile. 'Yes, I'm sure I'll feel like something in fifteen minutes or so.'

He locked the surgery and they left the hospital, locking its outer door securely as well, although the pager clipped to Dr Gray's belt meant that no emergency would escape his attention.

The lifts were in heavy use as arriving passengers and their luggage were transported to the five different decks where cabins were located. Jennie and Dr Gray were left waiting for several minutes. He said little during this time and somehow this only served to heighten the curiosity that she already felt about the senior medical officer.

For a start, why was he here? This was not exactly a recognised way-station along an ambitious career path. Hector had already made it quite clear what the attractions of the job were for him, and she suspected that there was financial incentive, too. In his homeland of Colombia, a doctor's pay was probably far less than it would be here aboard the *Leeward*. No such incentive would exist for Anthony Gray, and if he, too, were on the look-out for available female passengers he was far more discreet about it than Hector Mendez. . .

The lift arrived at last and they were swept upwards, pausing briefly at Deck Five to admit a lavishly dressed blonde whose hair, stiffly sculpted into an enormous and artistically tumbled coiffure, seemed to emit its own light. The woman saw Dr Gray, immediately noted the uniform and insignia of a ship's officer, let her gaze drift upwards to assure herself that he was of satisfactory height and gave him a dazzling smile. Anthony Gray returned the smile with as much emphasis as his professional courtesy required, but no more. The blonde departed at Deck Eight, disappointed.

Then he's not on the prowl, like Hector, Jennie decided to herself. That's a relief! Two of them would be a bit much. But then. . .why is he here? What is he hiding? He must be running away, like me. . .

It was three o'clock in the morning and the ward was very quiet. Jennie sat beside the bed of the indigent old man for whom nothing could now be done. Freddy Blount's bowel cancer had been discovered too late and exploratory surgery had revealed that it was only a matter of time before he died. It might well be tonight, and if it was Jennie wanted at least to do *something* to ease his last hours of consciousness. She wanted to be there, even though he no longer knew who anybody was.

In five minutes she would have to leave the old man, gently extricate her hand from his dry, feeble grip and make the rounds of the eight post-operative patients that were her responsibility tonight. But for the moment she could stay, and she did.

Old Mr Blount spoke. What was it? A name. 'Annie. . . Annie. . .'

'It's all right. I'm here,' Jennie said softly. Did he think that *she* was Annie? All the better if he did, probably.

'Annie. . .' It was a sigh of contentment. Who was Annie? No one had visited the old man at all during his week on the ward.

'Where are you, Annie, damn you?' Jennie muttered but perhaps Annie had died long ago. It seemed unlikely that anyone would ever know.

Her lightly imprisoned hand was sticky with warmth now. Just a few more minutes until she had to ——

'Sister McDougall? Sister McDougall! Come quickly! It's Sir Peter. Sister, I think he's dead!'

The other nurse's voice echoed like a nightmare, but the scene was real, relived again and again in Jennie's memory till it was mind-numbingly familiar.

She hurried after Alison Hartshorn, flung herself into Sir Peter Farrow's private room, checked his vital signs, and called for an emergency team while she frantically began resuscitation attempts herself. Too late. No use. A simple surgical procedure, a benign growth safely removed, no worrying signs while the patient was in post-operative recovery, and now, fifteen hours later, the man who had just endowed a new surgical wing at the Edgewater Grange Hospital was suddenly dead. A haemorrhage? A clot? A coronary? Only an autopsy would reveal the answer.

The scene in Jennie's memory shifted. Now it was dawn, her eyes were stinging with fatigue and she was alone in a tiny office with Ralph Caine. Ralph. Her fiancé of four months. She had just told him the story of the night from her own perspective and in her voice, she knew, there had been an open, trembling plea for his reassurance: There was nothing she could have done. Nothing anyone could have done. Sir Peter had been in no danger. No one could have predicted his death. She was *not* to blame! Of course easing the last hours of a lonely old man was more important than hanging over a post-operative patient whose minor surgery was only creating a fuss around the hospital because he was a VIP.

But Ralph Caine did not give this reassurance that she so despertely needed from him and no one else. Instead he rounded on her in blazing anger. Where were her priorities? Where was her concern for his career? Did she have any idea how much a connection with the man could have advanced him in the world of surgery? Sir Peter should not have been out of a nurse's sight for one moment. And where had Jennie been? With a nobody whom everyone knew was slated to die anyway.

Mr Blount *had* died, too, alone, half an hour after Jennie had left him, while the ward was still in an uproar over Sir Peter, and when another nurse had gone in and found the old man he had had a very calm, very faint smile on his face. . .

'I don't understand you, Jennie,' Ralph said stiffly, his classically handsome face reddened. 'I thought you were a complete professional. And I thought you understood my career goals.'

She had thought so, too, until today. She had loved and admired traits in him that she had labelled enthusiasm and dedication, had been excited by the energy with which he spoke of his ambitions and plans.

'My career goals'. He had never used those words about his future before. Words she would never forget, as she suddenly saw how much closer they were to the reality of how he viewed his world. They drummed in her head for the rest of that awful day, and by the end of it, with a pounding headache that seemed to throb to the rhythm of Ralph's voice. . .'I don't understand you, Jennie. . .' she knew that she had to break off their engagement.

Another shift of scene. Do it as soon as possible, she had decided. Don't make things worse by delaying. She asked to see him the next afternoon when they both had time off. They met at a café. Ralph still lived in his parents' sombre and over-furnished house when he was not on call and sleeping at the hospital, and she couldn't bear the idea of conducting their exchange in his mother's painfully neat, dark and expensive sitting-room.

So, a café. Crowded and steamy as it was a cold and
rainy early April day outside.

'I know you want to apologise. . .' Ralph's first stiff
words, so ludicrously off the mark that even now Jennie
almost laughed at the memory of them. He was fiddling
with the sugar, scooping up a spoonful and letting it
slowly trickle back into the glass bowl.

'Can you stop doing that, Ralph?'

'Oh. . .of course. Didn't realise it bothered you.' Of
course he didn't. She had never seen him do it before.

'I don't want to apologise,' she said steadily to him
now. 'I want to break off our engagement.'

And he didn't have a clue why she was saying it. He
argued, pointing out particulars. She had wanted him
to argue, of course. She wanted him suddenly to
become again the man she had been in love with. . .
and still was. . .someone who could be boyish and
endearingly naïve as well as earnest and alarmingly
intelligent. . .and cold. But the arguments he used only
made her feel worse. His mother would be so disappointed. She liked Jennie.

'She thinks you'll make a good, solid wife. And I do,
too. Jennie, I'm sorry if I was too angry yesterday, but
you must see. . . Damn it! I *am* angry! Sir Peter Farrow
is dead because of *your* twisted priorities. A brilliant
man, rich as hell, with years of philanthropy left in him
and you were holding hands with some drunken
old——'

Jennie rose at this, a stream of furious, miserable
words rising in her throat only to jam there behind a
growing lump of pain. 'Goodbye, Ralph,' was all she
managed to say as she twisted his solitaire emerald
painfully off the third finger of her left hand, tearing a
fingernail and grating her skin with it as she did so, and
leaving a small, cold circle of bare skin where the ring

had warmed her finger for four months in which she had sincerely believed herself to be happy.

She just had time to see Ralph's expression as he stared down at the bright circle of gold and green in his palm. On his lean, tidily proportioned face she saw anger, bewilderment, disbelief, impatience. What she couldn't discern at all, though, was pain or love.

Seconds later, she was pounding along the street in the rain, not caring that her thick halo of red curls was plastering itself more wetly and heavily to her head and shoulders every minute. 'I don't understand you, Jennie. . . Sir Peter Farrow is dead because of you. . . I don't understand you, Jennie'.

'This is a sheltered spot,' said Anthony Gray, placing a red tray on a moulded-plastic outdoor table. 'The wind is still a little chilly in spite of the sun breaking through now.'

Jennie followed his lead without speakig, still shaking off memories that were far too fresh and raw. She had wondered if Anthony Gray was running away from something. She knew now for certain that she was, and that it was vital that she do so. Doubting her professional and personal judgement as she now did, it would have been impossible to stay at Edgewater Grange.

And Ralph, of course, was still there. They had been forced to encounter each other many times in the two weeks while she waited for her resignation to take effect, and each time had come the feeling of betrayal as she saw a stranger's eyes looking out of the face of someone she had thought she loved.

How could I have been so wrong about him? That was a question she still hadn't answered. . . 'I can't get over this ship!' she exclaimed to Dr Gray now with determined enthusiasm, knowing it was time to seize

hold of this new life she had chosen for herself, instead
of dwelling on the past.

'Yes, this is one of my favourite times and places, up
here on deck when we sail.' The Englishman smiled
back at her. 'Unfortunately there's often too much to
do for me to be up here enjoying it.'

His colour was improving by the minute and he was
ready to eat now, picking up the roast beef and salad
sandwich from his plate and taking an appreciative bite.
There was a long line of passengers queuing for the
elaborate buffet now, but Jennie had followed Dr
Gray's lead — automatically, as she had still been
immersed in the painful reliving of her last weeks in
England — and joined a much smaller queue for a food
bar serving only sandwiches and fruit, tea and coffee.

The table he had chosen was sheltered by a wall of
plexiglass that ran around the entire perimeter of this
open deck. Two pools filled the centre of the space,
empty of water at this stage, and the blue outdoor
carpeting that surrounded them was crowded with
lounging-chairs, some already occupied by enthusiastic
tanners. Other passengers stood on a higher deck that
overlooked this one, leaning over the railings as they
enjoyed the New York skyline.

Now that the weather had improved a little, the city
did have a compelling beauty and excitement to it, with
its classic silhouette of skyward-reaching buildings and
canyon-like streets between. Hector Mendez's theatri-
cal reverence for the privilege of travel began to make
more sense and called forth a responsive chord in
Jennie.

She began to look through the manila folder that Dr
Gray had brought with him and which he now thrust
towards her. It contained a wealth of enticing detail
about her future shipboard life — everything from tourist pamphlets about Bermuda, where the *Leeward*

docked for nearly four days each week, to lists of pharmaceuticals kept in the hospital dispensary.

'We open for surgery hours between five and eight each afternoon as well as for three hours in the morning,' Dr Gray told her. 'Normally you and Sister Balasingham will take it in turns, as will Dr Mendez and myself, but for today I'd like you to be there with Tilly to learn the ropes.'

'That sounds sensible,' Jennie nodded.

'The worst thing about this job, as Tilly will tell you, is the paperwork.'

'Really? I'd have thought that——'

'Two reasons. First, the American health insurance system, since by far the majority of our passengers are American, and second, in this cynical age, the shipping company's desire to avoid lawsuits from passengers.'

'I should have expected that, I suppose.' She laughed, and caught the first full smile she had seen in the senior doctor's face.

It did wonders for him. Till now, she had considered his features and the planes of his high forehead and cheekbones too sombre, too immobile and cold. But this smile, breaking slowly over his face and drawing those well-shaped lips apart to reveal very white, even teeth, changed all that. Perhaps he wasn't a cold man at all. She thought of that hastily hidden letter, those teeth clenched with the pain of his migraine headache. . . Perhaps, on the contrary, his passions ran very deep.

'It's tempting to look at all the travel pamphlets first,' Jennie said now, wondering if she could tempt him into smiling once again, since she definitely liked the effect.

It worked. Those eyes crinkled at the corners again. But before he could reply, Jennie felt a light, caressing hand on her shoulder and turned to find Hector Mendez standing behind her chair. In one fluid movement he had pulled out a chair of his own and sat down, his knee brushing hers and resting there so that she could feel his warmth. . .until she gently drew her own leg away a little.

'Bermuda. . .' he said lazily. 'You have a bikini, I hope?'

'Not a bikini, but——'

'Too bad. You will let me take you to the beach on our day off, though, won't you?'

Jennie couldn't help laughing and tossing her red curls. The man was so brazen that she was in no danger whatsoever of taking his flirtation seriously. In fact, if she did, it would probably make him run a mile.

'If I have a day off in Burmuda, I'd love to go to the beach,' she said.

'Anthony, she has a day off in Bermuda, doesn't she?' Hector asked in a sleek, cajoling tone.

'You know very well that we all do, Hector,' the senior doctor said. The sombre mantle was back again now, to Jennie's disappointment. A moment of laughter, a glimpse of turquoise seas in the enticing tourist brochures, and, yes, even a completely meaningless flirtation with Hector Mendez. . . Gropingly, she understood that her bruised soul needed these things.

Anthony Gray had finished his lunch by this time, as had Jennie herself. He rose and said, 'Tilly must be back on board by now. Let me take you down and introduce her to you, Sister McDougall.'

'Please, if it's Tilly, can you make it Genevieve. . .or better, Jennie?'

He nodded curtly as he placed his tray on a wheeled waste trolley, but said nothing more. . .until they reached the lift, that was. As so many of the passengers were now settled in their cabins or enjoying the buffet, they had the mirrored compartment to themselves, and

Anthony Gray wasted no time in making use of the privacy.

'I hope you're not in danger of taking Hector at all seriously,' he said, as soon as the doors had silently closed. The slate-grey eyes flicked quickly up and down, assessing her appearance in a way she had not seen him do before. She found herself flushing at the frank and not particularly flattering scrutiny.

Is that what he thinks? That I'm expecting this job to be one long holiday romance? Did she give the impression of being so very eager and naïve? she asked herself.

In the full wall mirror of the lift she saw herself as he must be seeing her: compact build, clear blue eyes, the red curls that she never quite managed to tame as well as she wanted to, a light dappling of freckles laid over a creamy skin that turned to a pale, pretty gold in the sun but nothing darker.

Her clothes. . .could he find fault with those? Surely not. She wasn't dressed like an over-excited passenger. Jennie had taken note of the parade of jewels, the optimistically brief shorts and tops, the nautical motifs expressed in a wealth of navy and white sailor suits in silk and rayon. Having dressed to be comfortable on the aeroplane, Jennie wore a neat skirt in lemon-yellow gabardine, a white blouse and a matching lemon jacket. The skirt had a soft elastic waistband, her white shoes were flat-heeled and the modest collection of jewellery she had brought was stored securely in the white leather bag that swung from a shoulder-strap to her hip.

As for make-up. . .the little she had applied eleven hours ago in a nondescript London hotel had long ago disappeared. Eleven hours ago! Jennie suddenly realised that she was tired. And snappy. Anger hit in the few seconds it took to take in fully the import of Anthony Gray's comment, and when she replied it was with quite a bite.

'I'm not in any danger at all, Dr Gray.' Then a heavily sarcastic addition. 'But thank you very much for your concern for my virtue!'

She heard his hissing intake of breath and bit her lip. He was angry now, too. 'My concern,' he echoed with heavy emphasis, 'is not for your virtue. That's your own responsibility.'

'Is it? Thank you for telling me!'

'My concern is for your professional conduct while you are under my direction. Hector is a womaniser. . .'

'That's blunt.'

'It's accurate.'

'He certainly flirts. . .'

He ignored her, stepping out of the lift into the deserted corridors of Deck Three. 'And while the female passengers have to take care of themselves in that regard, I won't have one of my nurses in a state of lovelorn fog for the entire summer.'

'I don't intend to be in a lovelorn fog, Dr Gray, over Hector Mendez or anyone else,' she told him icily and quite truthfully. 'Not that's it's any of your business.'

'Good,' he snapped, ignoring her last phrase. 'Because this job. . . By the way, I won't enquire into your reasons for taking it. . .'

'You've already made it quite clear what you imagine to be my reasons for taking it.'

'If I'm wrong, so much the better, because this job, as I was saying, is not the cushy ride that some people assume. We sometimes have serious medical problems to deal with, and without the back-up of a major hospital system. Many of our passengers are elderly and many of them overdo it because they're on holiday and they're eating too much rich food. The paperwork is, as I have said, very demanding, and the company requires a meticulous inventory of all pharmaceuticals and other supplies to be made once a month.'

'Once a month?' she murmured, realising the work that this would entail.

He went on, 'With only one other nurse on rotation, you can find yourself up all night, with surgery hours the next day, and I guarantee that there will be at least one of your days off in Bermuda where you won't set foot on land, let alone get to those famous pink beaches, because you'll be curled up in your bunk catching up on three days of lost sleep.'

She glared at him and his grey eyes met hers unflinchingly. They had covered the length of the corridor quickly, each taking strides made more rapid by anger. Now they stopped. Hearing a noise from behind the bland door, marked '3002', and guessing that Tilly Balasingham was inside, Jennie lowered her voice to an emphatic hiss. 'You've made your point, Dr Gray. It wasn't necessary, but you've definitely made it.'

'I'm glad.' Nothing in his set face suggested gladness.

Beneath her anger, Jennie was disappointed. There had been one or two moments in his surgery and over lunch when she had thought that she might find a source of support in this fellow countryman, but the angry exchange between them, which seemed to have flared up out of nowhere, did not bode well. She had felt curious, earlier, as to his reasons for being here on the *Leeward*. Now she told herself that she couldn't care less.

When, again, she had trouble with the unfamiliar plastic key-card, and he took it from her with a brief, 'This way up,' his fingers brushed hers for a second and she pulled her hand quickly away, almost snatching at the key as she thanked him. She did not want the intimacy of his touch, however brief and accidental.

The door swung open and his murmured, 'Time for you to meet Tilly,' was very cool.

CHAPTER TWO

'Now is a good time to unpack,' Tilly Balasingham suggested to Jennie. 'If you are efficient, you will be done before we sail and can go up on deck.'

'Dr Gray wanted me to work with you tonight so you could show me the ropes,' Jennie answered uncertainly.

'It won't matter if you are a bit late,' the petite Filipino nurse assured her new cabin-mate. 'Enjoy the sight of New York Harbour while it's all new for you. The first evening is usually quiet anyway.'

They smiled at each other, the beginnings of a courteous friendship. The black-eyed nurse was dressed in her white uniform, which emphasised her deep olive skin and the glossy coil of black hair pinned neatly to the top of her head. She seemed nice, and her reserve and politeness came as a relief to Jennie.

'How long have you been on the *Leeward*?' the new nurse asked as she set a suitcase on the bed and began lifting out neatly laid-out and folded clothing.

'Since last October. I have just renewed my contract for another six months. The nursing contracts here are always for six months, the doctors have a nine-month contract.'

'You like it, then?'

'Of course. It's an opportunity for travel, meeting people, seeing something different.'

It was a bland answer, but seemed genuine enough. In any case, Jennie thought, I'm not going to quiz her.

Then, as if fearing that she had not said enough, Tilly added cautiously, 'I'm able to send a little money to my family at home each month, too,' and Jennie realised

26

that this was probably the most important thing for
Sister Balasingham.

Tilly said little more after this, sitting at the small
vanity table and writing postcards in a neat, precise
hand. Jennie was content to unpack and to keep her
thoughts to herself. She found that she was relieved at
Tilly Balasingham's evident reserve, having feared over
the past week or so that her fellow nurse might be some
chatty lass who would want nightly sessions of intimate
conversation, picking apart the doctors, the passengers
and crew. . . And, worse, full of questions about her
life in England, like, Had a boyfriend in Newcastle, did
you?

After unpacking Jennie had a shower, enjoying the
detachable shower rose on its long snake of metal hose
and deciding that this fully made up for the cramped
confines of the shower enclosure. She had just switched
off the plentiful water when a discreet tap sounded at
the bathroom door. 'We're sailing very soon, Jennie, if
you want to go up on deck. I can see them pulling up
the crew's gangway now.'

'Thanks!' she called and dived hastily into underwear
and a uniform, coming out of the bathroom to add
tights, flat white leather shoes and a light navy jacket.
Refreshed by the shower, she threw another smile to
Tilly and hurried up to the top deck.

Just in time. At first, she wasn't even sure that they
were moving, the ship's thrust out from the long wharf
was so slow and smooth. Then the space widened to
reveal a slice of murky harbour water and it was clear
that they were on their way. A Caribbean band played
steel drums on an open dais beyond the pool, the
cocktail bars were open and the deck was crowded with
people in holiday gear pointing and clicking cameras.

Jennie was caught by the mood and felt that she, like
the ship, was loosing her moorings and sailing off to a

freedom from the turmoil she had known over the past few weeks. As she found a space by herself at the ship's metal railing, Ralph's face appeared to her mind's eye, giving her a brief, stabbing pang of anger, hurt and loss, then the image dissolved and she thought only of the skyline that was slipping past, with its tantalising glimpses of the Chrysler building, the Empire State, the World Trade Center and finally, on the opposite side of the ship, Ellis Island and the Statue of Liberty.

There was something surprisingly beautiful about the busiest and most uncompromising of cities: the sculpted piles of buildings, the frank evidence of decay in parts, the sparkling reflections from façades made of the latest in smoky glass, and that well-known statue, dwarfed by the open, breeze-filled harbour but its focal point none the less.

Now the lower skyline of Brooklyn was passing, while ahead loomed a curved arc of bridge, spanning the Verrazano Narrows. The huge white ship slid silently beneath it and Jennie looked upwards to see its pattern of vertical cables silhouetted against a sky that was now blue and filled with billowing white clouds. The air was tangy with the smell of the sea now, and a slight swell began to tease the ship after the calm of the harbour. Their course would take them in a straight line almost seven hundred and fifty miles to the south-east across the open Atlantic. . .

As she felt the swell growing, Jennie knew the most breathtaking sensation of freshness and new beginning that she had ever felt, and then she looked down, saw her uniform whipping around her legs in the breeze and remembered that there was another side to all this. These passengers, drinking and laughing so carelessly around her, were here for a holiday. She was not.

Moments later, she had threaded her way through the crowded clusters of people and regained the quiet of the lift area. Impulsively, she decided not to wait for a lift but to take the stairs, twisting down seven flights until she emerged and saw the beige door of the ship's hospital, now open.

And all at once, without anticipating the reaction at all, she found that her legs were shaking and her stomach was heavy and queasy. Those last two weeks of work in Newcastle had passed in a slow daze of doubt and confusion. She had got through them only by gritting her teeth and working like a robot, several times having reluctantly to ask a colleague if she could exchange a difficult nursing task for an easier one and gaining even more concessions—concessions that she was quite unaware of at the time—through the look of strain and fear that seemed permanently etched on to her features.

'What's wrong with Sister McDougall?' Twice she had accidentally heard this whispered question from nurses who had not been on duty when Sir Peter Farrow had died, and twice she had caught the first faint whispered phrases of explanation before moving deliberately away:

'Sir Peter died on her shift. And I heard it's all off between her and Dr Caine.'

'Really? That'll put her nose out of joint!'

'Yes, he thinks she should have. . .'

Here on the *Leeward* there was no Ralph Caine, no patients recovering from surgery, no one who knew what had happened, and she hadn't expected that in this new environment the doubts and fears would all come back so strongly.

I can't do it, she thought in one desperate moment of panic. I can't!

Then Hector appeared in the doorway of the surgery with his lazy, superficial smile and an arm that immediately came round her shoulders to caress them lightly. 'So the uniform fits, I see. Ver-r-y nice!'

'Yes,' she managed, knowing in that moment that she *would* make a success of this. She *had* to.

'Not feeling seasick?' He cocked his head to one side and frowned.

'No.'

'Nervous, then,' he guessed accurately, his green eyes sparkling with their usual flirting warmth. 'Surely you're not the nervous type. . .?'

'Of course I'm not,' she spat out with sudden spirit.

He laughed lightly. 'There! That's better. Tilly, stop writing reports and. . .let's see. . .make your new friend a cup of coffee?' It was a question to Jennie as much as to Sister Balasingham.

Weakly, she nodded, and Tilly rose with a neat smile. 'How do you like it?'

'I'll do it,' Jennie offered quickly. 'If you'll just show me where everything is.'

'Everything' was not much. In the first of the hospital's four tiny wards there was a sink, an electric jug, some mugs, sugar, teabags and instant coffee. Jennie, who liked lots of milk in hers, was told to ring Room Service. Five minutes later, a Polish-accented cabin steward appeared with a small carton placed neatly all by itself in the centre of a napkined silver tray and Jennie took it, trying not to laugh at the formality of the offering. The *Leeward* certainly provided luxury service.

Making the coffee, for Hector and Tilly as well as herself, was just the mechanical task she needed. That, and her amusement at the arrival of the milk, eased Jennie into the new situation and out of a state of nervousness and panic that had been quite foreign to her temperament until recently.

It wasn't until half-past five that they had their first patients.

'Seasick,' murmured Tilly, rising from the desk in the dispensary which the nurses used as a sort of office.

'How can you tell?'

But Tilly had gone forward to the elderly couple who were making their tentative way across the waiting-room.

'Can I help?' The petite nurse's Filipino accent was melodious.

'We thought the waiting-room would be full,' the woman said, shaking her silver-blue head in surprise. 'This is pretty rough, isn't it?'

Her husband looked tentative and surprised, too.

'No,' Tilly said, 'I'm afraid it's not rough at all. This is a very gentle swell.'

'Oh, dear, it's our first cruise, our first time at sea. . .' the elderly woman explained.

Tilly reached for a small carton on a shelf in the dispensary and took out several little packets of a seasickness remedy, then knocked on Hector's door. 'The doctor will want to talk to you, but this is what he'll have you take, I should think.'

'I've heard something about a patch that goes behind your ear, and the medicine gets absorbed through the skin. . .' the husband said.

'We don't recommend that here. It has some side-effects that we are not comfortable with,' said Hector, with immediate authority, as he appeared in the door-way. 'Come in! You poor things! Already. Let's see. . .' The door closed behind him and the couple.

'You have more than one kind of remedy here,' Jennie said, glancing at the shelf.

'Yes,' Tilly nodded. 'Depending on the severity of the symptoms and on any other medication they are taking.'

'I must say I'm not noticing the swell much yet myself.'

'Good. It would be bad luck for you if you were, because this is very slight.'

'Do you get seasick?'

'Just once I did, in February on the return trip from Bermuda after a big storm. Horrible!'

'I've heard it is.'

'If you feel it coming on, go on deck, if you can, get some fresh air. And *eat* something!'

A few moments later the couple came out of the surgery, clutching their cachets of medication and bestowing warm smiles on Tilly and Jennie.

'Don't forget to eat,' Sister Balasingham reminded them. They nodded doubtfully at this and left.

'Oh, dear!' said Jennie.

'Fortunately we have three nights and four days at anchor in Bermuda. They shouldn't suffer too much.'

'We don't charge for a consultation on seasickness?'

'No,' Tilly answered. 'The paperwork is already bad enough. If we tried to record every passenger or crew member who came in with that problem we would be drowning under an ocean of forms.'

'I don't like that metaphor much, somehow,' Jennie said.

'Sorry,' Tilly laughed.

No other passengers came in for seasickness that night. The two nurses had a quiet twenty minutes going over record systems and Tilly, looking at her watch and finding that it was now six o'clock and time for the first seating of the passengers' dinner, predicted that no one else would come until just before their hours were over. At that moment, though, the phone rang in the dispensary.

Tilly's voice was calm as she spoke into the receiver, but when she put the phone down she made an expres-

sive face with her small features. 'Better page Dr Gray,'
she said. 'There's a little boy coming in. The parents
think he has dislocated his shoulder.'

Moments later an anxious American couple entered
the waiting-room, the frantic mother cradling a two-
year-old who was crying loudly and was evidently in
some pain. Hector came out of his office at once.
Taking the child, he began crooning to it, ignoring the
screams that became even louder. Manipulating the
arm briefly, he nodded.

'Yes, there is something. We'll have to X-ray it to
make sure.'

Tilly responded immediately to his words and went
to prepare the machine and the photographic plates. It
was heart-breaking to watch the little boy's struggles as
he was made to lie on this strange contraption that he
did not understand.

'How did it happen?' Dr Mendez asked the couple.

'We don't know,' the husband confessed, and the
wife broke in,

'That seems so terrible.'

'He was with my mother, and she was swinging him,
then she tried to pick him up and he went limp and
started crying.'

'She thought he was crying for me,' the mother said.
'I was in our cabin and he's going through a very clingy
stage.'

'She brought him down and at first we tried to
comfort him. . .'

'Then I saw how he was holding his arm. . . How
could I not have seen at once that he was in pain?' Mrs
Wolsky said, wringing her hands.

Hector nodded rather absently at the parents'
anguished account and looked twice towards the open
door of the small X-ray room, clearly hoping that
Anthony Gray would soon arrive. He motioned to the

fair-haired little boy's parents to leave the room and
had Jennie hold the button that activated the X-ray
while he held the small blue-eyed Jonathan in the
correct position.

Jennie pressed the button on his command, then they
turned Jonathan over and took another picture from a
different angle, hoing that the crying child had been
still enough to create a clear picture. Hector then
looked towards the door again. Jennie wasn't nearly so
anxious to encounter the senior doctor again, after their
angry words and terse parting a few hours ago. . .

However he came, of course, inevitably, and it did
no good to wish that Hector had commandeered Tilly's
assistance with this instead of her own. Tilly was now
talking to the little boy's parents out in the waiting-
room and had barely had time to smile at the senior
doctor as he came striding through the open office and
into the X-ray room.

'Got the pictures?'

'Yes,' Hector said. 'We'll look at them, but it seems
the parents are right. A dislocated shoulder.'

Jennie picked up the crying and exhausted child,
holding him as gently as she could so that his arm was
not made any more painful. Anthony stepped forward
and spoke sharply. 'Is that how he's been holding it all
along?'

'Yes.' Jennie nodded quickly. She was not sure why
the senior doctor had asked the question but she
remembered that in his parents' arms, too, Jonathan
had held his arm flat against the front of his body, the
elbow bent at a right angle.

'Hmm,' was all the Englishman said. Was he still as
angry as all that about this afternoon?

She waited while the two doctors studied the X-rays
together. She didn't have to wait long. Anthony Gray
was quick and decisive in reaching his verdict. 'Dislo-

cated, yes, Hector. But not the shoulder. It's his elbow. A shoulder dislocation would have flung the arm backwards. I'll show you some diagrams later.'

Hector nodded, his honey-tanned cheeks suddenly a little flushed. It was clear now that Anthony Gray's status as the more senior doctor was not merely a formality. He did not flaunt his superior knowledge, however, and Hector soon relaxed again.

'Let's give him a tranquilliser and get that joint manipulated back into place. He's been in pain for long enough.'

Instructing Hector to prepare a syringe, Dr Gray went quickly back to the waiting-room and brought in Mr and Mrs Wolsky, not waiting for anxious questions from them before explaining exactly what would be done. Poor little Jonathan's screams redoubled as an injection was administered, then soon he grew drowsy and was taken into the tiny operating-room where full anaesthesia was available.

'We may not need it,' Anthony Gray said. 'I'm going to try manipulating the arm gently through its range of motion first. With any luck this tranquilliser will relax him enough to——'

He didn't finish, working the small arm as he spoke while Hector stood by with anaesthesia and Jennie helped to hold the boy on the table. In spite of the medication, he was still struggling and crying, and after only a moment or two Anthony shook his head and motioned to Hector, who put the gas mask over the boy's nose and mouth to send him briefly into unconsciousness. At last the cries were silenced and in a few expert movements Anthony had worked the elbow back into place. He nodded to Hector again and the mask was removed.

'Bring him out to his parents, Jennie, he's waking up already.'

'Dr Gray. . .?' He was stepping ahead to open the door, turning back at the query in her tone. 'He'll probably be nauseous, won't he?'

'Yes. Keep him near the sink. He's exhausted, poor love. . .'

Suddenly, and very surprisingly, he put out a hand and gave the drowsy, tear-stained little face the softest and tenderest of touches, then opened the second door that led from the operating-room. 'You'll immobilise the arm and shoulder with bandage, Hector, and tell the parents to bring him back the day after tomorrow, when we dock in Bermuda.'

He left on this note, and Jennie didn't have time to wonder at what had just been revealed about the man. Jonathan was still struggling in her arms, albeit drowsily, and when he saw his mother he held out his hands to her and began to gag almost immediately as the effect of his brief anaesthesia came over him. He cried again, of course, but a few minutes later it was all over and Hector was able to put a long pink stretchy bandage around chest, shoulder and arm, effectively immobilising it against the toddler's side.

Mr and Mrs Wolsky were pale and shaky, with many questions still unanswered. Hector was upbeat and reassuring, taking a generous amount of time to make sure everything was explained. Jennie liked his bedside manner, and in the end he even coaxed a trembling laugh from Mrs Wolsky. 'He'll sleep for twelve hours tonight. You'd better get a cabin steward to baby-sit for you while you go to the casino.'

'Yes, look, Nina, he's almost asleep now,' Mr Wolsky said.

The child nestled against his mother's shoulder, his creamy eyelids growing heavier and heavier. He had been too drowsy to protest against the confining bandage, and now, from his expression of peaceful exhaustion, no one could have guessed how recently he had been in pain.

'Thank goodness it's over,' Mrs Wolsky whispered, cuddling him tightly and covering the fine straight hair, fluffed into a fuzzy halo, with fervent kisses. At rest like this, he was an adorable little boy, with a soft button of a nose, thick dark lashes and smooth baby cheeks.

'Is Dr Gray still here?' Mr Wolsky wanted to know as Jennie ushered the family out. In the background, Tilly was busy with a new Romanian crew member who was complaining of seasickness.

'No, he had to attend to something else,' Jennie improvised quickly, thinking again of that surprisingly tender touch and the abrupt departure that had followed it.

The Wolskys nodded, quite satisfied at this explanation, and then they had gone. Surgery hours were almost at an end for the evening by this time. Tilly and Hector had soon dispatched the seasick crew member, and no one else came in. With her body clock still set on London time, Jennie was starting to think longingly of that freshly made bed in her new cabin. 'But you must eat something,' Hector insisted, piloting both her and Tilly through to Deck Three's officers' mess, after they had closed the surgery.

'Just soup,' Jennie insisted, not attracted by the steaming piles of steak or chicken that she saw on many of the Greek shipping officers' plates.

The creamy vegetable soup was so delicious, though, that she ate three bowls of it, as well as a small salad. The officers' mess was rather warm and stuffy. Heavy, too, with the strong fumes of Greek tobacco, and she wasn't surprised as she finished her meal when Tilly noticed her flushed cheeks and heavy eyes and advised, 'Go up on deck, if your head is feeling woolly. Of course you are exhausted but you will sleep better for some fresh air and a stretch of your legs. I'm on call during the night, so if you hear the telephone later on in your sleep please try not to take any notice.'

'Thanks,' Jennie answered. 'And you're right about the fresh air.'

'You'll probably find Tony up there,' Hector came in as he rose from a hearty meal. 'He shares the English mania for fresh air.'

'And you, Hector?' It was a light query, but his words had disconcerted Jennie. She hoped that she *wouldn't* find Anthony Gray prowling the decks tonight.

'Me, I like the casino. There it smells of money. . . and women's perfume.' The junior doctor laughed brazenly, enjoying the effect of his exit line.

Jennie and Tilly raised their eyebrows at one another, and then Jennie asked in a low voice, 'Is he really as bad as he makes out?'

Tilly shrugged and glanced at the compact figure of the Colombian doctor as he made his way out of the mess. 'I'm afraid he is. But what can one say or do? I don't think he makes any false promises to these women. He just expects them to understand the rules. . .'

'And most of them do?'

'Fortunately, yes.'

'It takes all sorts to make a world, doesn't it?'

'Indeed!'

A few minutes later, Jennie had wrapped herself in a warm, windproof jacket and was on her way up to the deck. It was very quiet at this hour, in contrast to its crowded and noisy state this afternoon as the ship had steamed out of New York Harbour. Night had fallen, and a brisk wind brought cold air swooping down to ruffle the waters of the newly filled swimming pool.

One or two crew members were busy cleaning the pool surrounds, but the passengers were all below, some still enjoying the second seating of dinner while others watched the live variety show or played bingo, roulette and blackjack.

Jennie decided on the traditional shipboard exercise programme of circling the deck beside the railings. Tilly had been right to suggest the idea. The kind of stuffy tiredness that would have resulted in a throbbing headache developing during the night was soon replaced by a healthier, more genuine weariness.

A headache. . . Even as she thought about it she caught sight of the tall figure standing with face full in the wind at the *Leeward's* bow, as if his head still needed clearing. She recognised Anthony Gray at once, not surprised to see him after Hector's comment, but wishing in vain that she had not been so curious about seeing the ship's bridge. It was this curiosity that had made her climb a deck to look in at the raised arc of windows that commanded a wide view of the ocean before them.

Perhaps if I pretend I haven't seen him, pretend I'm so curious about craning up to the bridge to see if the captain is there. . .

No use. He had turned and seen her, calling above the wind, 'So you're a deck prowler, too? Come over here. The railing is high and solid at this point. It's more sheltered.' His glance took in the white cotton skirt of her uniform which was inadequate and flapped against her legs, threatening to whirl upwards in a sudden gust.

'All right. Thanks.' She came over, still very wary of the man.

'How is little Jonathan?' he wanted to know at once.

'He was asleep in his mother's arms by the time they left. Hector was planning to look in at their cabin straight after dinner.' Then she couldn't help adding in a slightly accusing tone, 'Mr and Mrs Wolsky asked about you. I think they wanted to thank you. I told them you had something else to attend to.'

He studied her for a moment without speaking, then said very mildly, 'Did you? Thanks.'

He had taken the wind from her sails. . .and had relieved her at the same time. They had already been through one run-in today, and any sensible person *without* a red-headed temper wouldn't have risked provoking another. She didn't know what to say to him after this, wondered whether he wanted her to go or stay, and after a moment found that she was actually enjoying being here.

Her lower half was sheltered and her head was whipped into fresh wakefulness by the wind. With a half-moon in the sky, the sea was bright enough to sparkle with a blue light, and the swell that rolled ahead of them was hypnotic as it moved. Anthony seemed to be absorbed in thought. He leant his elbows on the flat metal railing and leaned forward so that she could see his dark hair whipping in the wind and feel a small buffer of warmth and shelter in the form of his jacketed left arm.

'Hector says you do this often,' she began, suddenly wanting to find some kind of meeting point with this enigmatic man.

But he ignored her opening and spoke slowly, and she knew that his thoughts must have been travelling towards this speech all along. 'I always planned to work with children,' he said. 'I wanted to specialise in neo-natal surgery. In fact, I trained for it for quite a while, working under Stephen Greer in London.'

Jennie hadn't heard of Stephen Greer, but she knew that the field of surgery on new-born infants was exceptionally demanding. What on earth was Anthony Gray doing *here*? He went on speaking.

'But we both realised after four years that I didn't have the temperament for it. When a patient is too young to respond except with those heart-rending cries of pain. . . Techniques in neonatal surgery are being refined all the time. Babies are growing to live normal healthy lives now when only a few years ago they would have died. It's a wonderful field to be in. . .but I couldn't do it. I still have some trouble occasionally with a young child in pain. They don't *understand*, you see.'

'But they don't remember, either,' Jennie reminded him gently. 'That's the blessed thing about pain, for adults as well as children. Think how strongly the memory of a familiar scent can be at times. Pain isn't like that. It fades. . . And I'm sorry I was accusing you of—'

'No,' he cut in firmly. '*I'm* sorry. About the way I rounded on you earlier. It's been a bad day. That migraine really rocked me. I hadn't had one for two months, and I was hoping. . . But never mind. The upshot of it is that I shouldn't have jumped to conclusions about you.'

'I over-reacted as well,' Jennie conceded. 'I think it was jet-lag. Funny, I felt exhausted before, but now. . .'

'No, Jennie,' he came in. 'Now you're *still* exhausted, but your body has tricked you with some kind of second wind. Better go below and get some sleep. I've put you on evening surgery hours tomorrow, as well as overnight call. After that, you'll want to enjoy your day off in Bermuda. We'll all tell you the same thing: snatch your sleep when you can.'

As if his words were not enough, he put out a hand

and turned her away from the railing then propelled
her forward with a light touch in the small of her back.

'Goodnight,' she managed, her voice scarcely carrying against the wind.

'Sleep well.' It reached her only as a murmur,
although he had probably spoken quite loudly.

Looking back just before she rounded the corner of
the bridge, she saw that he had already turned to stare
out to sea again. Funny. . . What he had told her
tonight about his past career ought to have left her
feeling that she knew more about the man. In fact, it
was the opposite. His words had only served to provoke
more unanswered questions, and she felt now that he
was more of a mystery than ever.

Did Dr Gray know just quite what a dark horse he
seemed? Jennie wondered. . .

CHAPTER THREE

IT WAS a glorious day. Jennie waited for Hector
Mendez near the gangway that led ashore from Deck
Three, watching brightly dressed groups of travellers
leaving the ship, many of them armed with beach gear
and most carrying cameras. She was dressed for the
beach herself, in a pale straw sunhat, a floral print dress
and open-toed sandals, with her swimsuit — and towels
provided by the ship — in a roomy canvas beach-bag.

Hector had suggested yesterday at lunch that they
meet here at a quarter to ten for the outing he had
promised her. Catching sight of a man's watch as he
passed by, Jennie saw that it was already nearly ten,
and she wondered if she had misunderstood the
arrangement. Surely not! True, her head was a little
fuzzy this morning.

On call last night with Dr Gray, she had been woken
twice from a sound sleep. The first time it had been to
help dress and suture a deep cut sustained by one of the
cooks while carving decorative fruits for the *Leeward's*
regular midnight buffet, and she had been able to return
to bed after only a short while.

Later in the night, though, at about four, they had
admitted a patient to their tiny hospital ward, complaining of chest pain, and after this she had only been able
to doze intermittently in the adjoining room. Thinking
back to yesterday, she reviewed the plan she had made
with Hector. No, he had definitely said Deck Three, by
the gangway at nine forty-five. Could there be a medical
emergency? she began to wonder.

From here she could see along the corridor in the

direction of the hospital, but could not see whether its door was open or shut. Her on-call time had ended at nine, and surgery hours would begin any minute, with Tilly and the senior doctor rostered on. As far as she knew, everything was going smoothly. Dr Gray had examined and discharged their overnight patient earlier this morning, with instructions to spend a quiet day aboard ship and return for another check-up this evening.

Has Hector overslept? Jennie thought. Should I go and knock on his cabin door?

She realised that she had not seen him at dinner last night, nor at breakfast this morning. The two doctors' cabins, one each and larger than that of the nurses, were along this same corridor, although she didn't know exactly which door belonged to Dr Gray. It would be a simple matter to. . .

The lift gave a bright ping as its doors opened to discharge another colourful flock of people from the higher decks and there, at last, was Dr Mendez. Jennie took a step forward, smiling brightly. She really was looking forward to this day! Then she stopped. Hector was not alone. No, indeed. Far from it!

A tanned blonde, well past the age of consent, draped herself possessively, almost hungrily on his arm and he was rewarding her attention with the most luxurious of smiles and some murmured, caressing words very close to her ear. That stiff, almost tinsel-like cloud of hair. . . Jennie realised that Hector's companion was the woman who had smiled at Anthony Gray and had assessed him so openly two days ago in the lift. It seemed that she had found the uniformed officer she had been seeking for her shipboard romance. . .

Only Hector wasn't in uniform today. He was

dressed, like nearly everyone else — and rather flamboy-
antly, too, in tropical print — for the beach.

The crowd had flooded from the lift now, with Hector
and his blonde the last to get out. Jennie stood frozen,
still not quite sure what to think. Then it became clear.
Hector swept past her, the American woman still on his
arm. She was pointing at the line of buildings that stood
opposite the wharf, and Hector just had time to catch
sight of Jennie, shrug covertly at her and give a helpless
smile as if the whole situation was regrettable. . .and
delicious. . .and quite beyond his control. The smile
contained a note of complicity, too, that said, You
know how these things are, and I've certainly stumbled
on to a good one this time, haven't I?

Then Hector and his new love-interest were on their
way up the gangway and out of sight.

He's stood me up, Jennie realised, still scarcely
believing it. She almost had to laugh. . .but not quite.
She had told herself that she was immune to the
Colombian doctor's superficial charm and it was true,
but he was fun to talk to and she had been looking
forward to their day. He had said that he knew the
island well. It would be like having her own private
tour guide.

Jennie was resourceful enough to find her way to the
beach alone, of course, but since she hadn't *planned* to
be alone she hadn't prepared for it and would have to
return to her cabin to dig out and study the tourist
pamphlets Anthony Gray had given her on Saturday.

Anthony. . . As she heard a familiar English voice
saying her name beside her, resonant and deep, she
realised that she had been in rather a daze. How long
had the senior doctor been standing there, trying to
attract her attention?

Long enough, it seemed. 'I take it he didn't let you
know he'd found Miss Right-for-this-week in the

Mariner's Club Bar yesterday afternoon?' he queried quite gently.

'No,' Jennie managed through a tight throat. It was so rude, and so sudden! Hector *could* have left her a note!

'A lot of people think Horseshoe Bay is the nicest of the beaches. It's in South Shore Park, easy to get to by bus. The terminal is on Washington Street, just along Front Street and up the hill,' he told her now, with a careful kindness that somehow made her feel worse. Then he added, as if it was merely an afterthought, 'Hector usually goes to Elbow Beach.'

'Thanks. I might go back to my cabin, though, and get out a tourist map before I set off. I hate getting lost!' She summoned a bright smile that didn't fully reach her blue eyes.

About to turn back down the corridor, she then felt his hand on her forearm in a light, restraining grip. 'Hey. . . You didn't get a lot of sleep last night, did you?'

'Not enough, no.'

'I heard Tilly say at breakfast that she would have preferred today off. Something about some embroidery silk that she's itching to pick up from a craft boutique as soon as possible. Perhaps it's not too late for you to swap rosters. We should be pretty quiet during the day today.'

'No seasickness, anyway!' she laughed.

'You can grab a long snooze this afternoon, cross your fingers for a quiet on-call tonight, and. . .'

'Be more refreshed and better prepared to go off exploring by myself tomorrow. Yes, if Tilly would do it, that would be so much better.'

Her spirits lifted, and she wanted to thank him for his perception and flexibility, but he was already striding in the direction of the hospital. 'Five past ten,' he said. 'I'd better open up, if Tilly hasn't done so already.'

Jennie followed him, and they had almost reached the hospital door when he suddenly stopped, turned to her and said quietly, 'Look, it's up to you, but there's no need to go alone tomorrow if you don't want to. I'd be very happy to take Hector's place.'

'I couldn't let you——'

'There's no "letting" about it. I've spent too many of my days off on this island alone.'

'All right, then,' she agreed, curious about him again.

Why had he been alone? Not through necessity, surely! Tilly spent quite a bit of time with some of the ship's hospitality staff—the casino workers, the boutique and gym staff, the social directors. Anthony Gray could easily have done the same, with attractive women of several nationalities to choose from if it was specifically female companionship that he was looking for. And yet he had kept himself to himself. Now he was talking about taking her out tomorrow as if it was some milestone in a process of recovery.

Yes! A flash of insight told her that this was exactly what it was. For a moment, she resented this, then asked herself sensibly if this wasn't exactly what she was doing herself. Not in her tentative new relationship with Anthony Gray necessarily, but in her whole life aboard the *Leeward*. The new understanding brought her closer to the senior doctor.

Tilly had already opened up the hospital when they arrived, and agreed with alacrity to the change in roster. She hurried off immediately, and would take over tomorrow at ten. As Anthony had predicted, it was a quiet morning. After changing into her white uniform, Jennie spent it in looking over some case-notes from earlier in the season, while Anthony seemed to be busy with reports. The Wolsky family were their earliest patients.

'Jonathan has been so good with that bandage,' Nina Wolsky said. 'I thought he'd try to pull it off, but he seems to understand that it's important.'

'He *can* have it off now,' Dr Gray pronounced. 'He's been in no pain or discomfort, has he?'

'Hasn't shown any signs of it,' Mr Wolsky came in.

'As active as ever,' his mother sighed.

Anthony manipulated the arm gently, while the little boy was surprisingly co-operative. He seemed to trust the doctor now, as if he had some inkling that Anthony had stopped his pain the other day. 'Feels fine,' the latter said after a few moments.

'Will there be any permanent weakness in the joint? Is it likely to slip out again?' Mr Wolsky asked.

'It shouldn't do. Be very careful of holding him in any way that twists those arms, though. Don't pick him up or swing him by the arms. And don't hold his hand and pull him one way if he's trying with all his might to go the other.'

'Hmm. . .'

'I know,' he nodded. 'Easier said than done with an independent two-year-old. Try a harness around his torso, if you have to. Not one of those dog-leash-type contraptions that fasten round his wrist, though.'

'But it's all right for him to swim at the beach today?'

'With my blessing. . .and with block-out cream and a sunhat. Get going before you miss the best of the day!'

The family left, and Anthony and Jennie had coffee together, talking a little more about medical matters. Three more patients trickled in, all with minor problems, and then one o'clock came and the surgery was closed.

The ship was very quiet today. Looking out of the small round porthole in her cabin after lunch, Jennie could see that the tourist boutiques on Front Street, just yards from the wharf, were doing a brisk trade in souvenir T-shirts and knick-knacks, Scotch whiskies and fine textile goods. Then she closed the curtains and settled down to sleep, waking at four in time to freshen up and enjoy afternoon tea before starting surgery hours again at five.

This time, they were inundated with patients. Three people had fallen from their rented scooters and sustained gravel grazes — 'road rash', the medical staff called these — or strained ligaments. 'No concussions, fortunately,' Dr Gray murmured to Jennie at one point. 'Helmets are compulsory here, but not everyone deigns to obey the law.'

Several people had spent too long in the sun while clad in too little and had severe cases of sunburn. And there was one fairly unpleasant young Canadian named Steve Waxman who had drunk too much beer, fallen asleep on the beach and was now so dehydrated that he had to be admitted to the ward and given intravenous fluids as well as being treated for severe sunburn and mild heat exhaustion.

He had been discharged again by the time they were ready to close at just after eight, but Anthony warned Jennie, 'During the night we're likely to get more of the same. Sun and scooters. Some people won't realise until later just how badly burned or bruised they are, and others won't be back on the ship yet.'

'In other words. . .'

'Don't worry, it usually dies down by about midnight.'

And in fact the night was quieter than Dr Gray had predicted, with their last beach- and bike-related injury turning up at a quarter-past eleven, and much later, near dawn, a mild facial burn to dress for one of the cooks, who had been splashed by some hot fat while preparing breakfast early in the morning.

Snatching some early breakfast herself in the officers' mess, after the Portuguese cook had been sent on his way, Jennie then shamelessly returned to bed for two hours, dozing intermittently and reading the historical novel she had borrowed from the ship's library. . .

Almost ten o'clock. Another glorious day. With vivid images of yesterday's sunburn cases before her mind's eye, Jennie had packed high-factor block-out cream in her beach-bag to protect her fair Scottish skin. Waiting by the gangway where she had waited yesterday, it seemed like *déjà vu* to see Hector emerging from the lift.

This time, though, he was alone and dressed in uniform ready for the day's surgery hours with Tilly. He looked a little sunburnt himself, and more than a little bleary-eyed. Catching sight of Jennie, his manner became a mixture of sheepishness and knowingness. He came up to her.

'Believe me, I'm grateful about yesterday. I knew you would understand. . .'

Jennie didn't bother to point out that she understood only too well, and that it *wasn't* something he should be grateful about.

'Corinne and I. . .we have a really wonderful connection together. We talk, we. . .'

'What a pity you're on duty today, then, isn't it?' she answered him tartly, strongly wanting to explode into a much more fulsome rage and tell the man a few home truths, but feeling even more strongly that to do so would be beneath her dignity.

'No, no,' Hector was saying, trying to disarm her with a light touch on her shoulder. 'You must never think that I do not take *that* part of my life seriously. You see, it is all part of the same thing. My reverence for life, you understand, as a doctor. . .and as a very passionate man.'

But she couldn't forgive him yet. 'Perhaps in future you could learn to take a few minutes out of your very passionate schedule to write a note of explanation when you find yourself forced to break a previous commitment.'

He laughed lightly and unrepentantly, then caught sight of Anthony Gray coming along the corridor from his cabin. Guessing immediately that Jennie and the senior doctor had arranged an outing, he murmured, 'You see, after all it is for the best.' His fluid Colombian accent had a cat-like purr. 'The two Britishers can now spend the day together and commiserate with one another on the terribleness of foreigners.'

Then he turned on his heel and headed at a quick and nimble pace down the far corridor, jangling his bunch of hospital keys in one hand. Since it was still only five minutes to ten, his retreating form must have looked, to the approaching Dr Gray, commendably responsible and conscientious.

'Ready?' said the Englishman as he came up to Jennie.

'Quite ready, thanks.'

Today, she hadn't needed to have him address her twice. She was fuming at Hector's last comment and couldn't get away from the man fast enough. All the way up the gangway, along the wharf and through the formality of the customs depot in its pink stucco building, she felt like a steam boiler about to blow a gasket and it wasn't until she heard the surprising sound of Anthony Gray's laughter beside her that she realised she hadn't spoken a word to the man since that first brief greeting.

'What's funny?' she bit out suspiciously.

His laughter, which, like his smile, seemed to come

too rarely, was a rich, full-bodied sound. 'You are!' he exclaimed, not in the least perturbed at her manner. 'What on earth did Hector say to you?'

The steam boiler exploded. 'He *said* that you and I would be bound to enjoy our day because as two typically insular Britons we could bitch about bloody foreigners to our hearts' content. Excuse the language!'

'He said all that?'

'No, I'm exaggerating a bit and I'm afraid the profanity is all mine, but I'm just so damned *angry* with him! Turning it into *my* fault! *My* problem! Hector could be from Tierra del Fuego or Clapham Junction or Buckingham Palce for all I care. Breaking an arrangement without telling me is *rude*!'

Maddeningly. . .and very refreshingly. . .he laughed even more at this, throwing his head back so that dark hair fell away from his forehead and exposed its smooth planes. Jennie's anger vanished into the air—the boiler's last puff of steam.

'Better now?' the doctor queried gently. That full top lip of his gave his face a very sensitive look when it was set in serious lines.

'Mmm, yes. Too nice a day to waste in anger.'

'Much too nice. You do have a temper, don't you, Jennie?'

'Not surprised, are you? Matches my hair. It's a well-known fact that all redheads are like that.'

'Another sore point? That you're a cliché?'

'Not really. It can be useful. Gives people fair warning. Especially careless student nurses. They only need to get one taste of it and they're suddenly *much* more hard-working. "Look at that hair!" they whisper to each other. "We should have known she had a temper!" Of course it doesn't work so well if it's the director of nursing I happen to explode at. I take it you're not cursed in the same way?'

'Or blessed. . .no. You flame. I smoulder.'

'Not good for your health.'

'I know. You're lucky if you don't bottle things up. I'm willing to bet you've never had a migraine in your life.'

'No, not migraines.' Suddenly they were both a little more serious. 'But you're wrong if you think that having a temper saves someone from bottling things up. I do it. I've done it. About the most important things.' She was thinking, of course, about Sir Peter Farrow's death. . .and Ralph.

'Well, take it from me, Hector Mendez is not worth smouldering over.'

'No, just a nice refreshing flare-up to clear the air. The air *is* clear today, isn't it?'

'Yes, less humid than it often gets later in the season. Now. . .ready for your first scooter ride?'

'Scooter?' The exclamation was a little horrified. After seeing those grazed arms and thighs and those strained ligaments yesterday. . .

'Don't worry, I've done this before,' he reassured her. 'You'll ride on the back and we'll both wear helmets, as we're supposed to. It's mostly Americans who get into trouble on mopeds and scooters because they're not used to driving on the left-hand side of the road. They panic.'

'Then we might see people careering towards us on the wrong side of the street shrieking their heads off?'

'Possibly. Trust me to bail us out?'

'I'll have to, won't I?'

They stopped at a scooter-rental place just along the street from the wharf, and Anthony was soon wheeling a natty little red and white machine out of its parking spot. 'Hop on, and hold tight.'

'Hold? On to what?'

'Me.'

At first she tried to get away with simply resting her
fingertips lightly on his hips but he was insistent. 'Arms
round my waist, can you? If I have to do something
sudden and unexpected, you could go flying a lot
quicker than you think. I'm sorry if you can't see.
Later, when you're used to it and when I'm more
comfortable with your weight, you can loosen up and
look around.'

Jennie didn't explain that not catching the view was
not her principal concern. It was the unexpected intimacy of the situation. She really did have to wrap her
arms around him, and if she *did* want to see the sights
they passed she had to turn her head to one side and
rest her cheek against the solid shape of his lower
shoulderblade. His back, clad in a soft cotton shirt of
tropical blue, was warm and so was the waist where
close-fitting and very casual blue jeans ended snugly in
a brown leather belt. Disconcertingly warm, disconcertingly pleasant.

As they left the busy, tourist-filled town of Hamilton,
the movements of the scooter turning and twisting along
narrow, winding streets made his back move against
her breasts and abdomen like a massage, and she could
feel the taut strength of his muscles. Stronger and more
taut, actually, than she would have expected in a man
whose job was not a very physical one. Once again, this
hinted at mystery. . .which was a far safer subject to
dwell on than her awareness of his palpably masculine
physique.

Finally, however, it was not Anthony Gray who filled
her thoughts. They left the town of Hamilton behind,
passed a beige-pink building set high on their left which
he shouted to her was the island's King Edward
Memorial Hospital, and then she became captivated by
the houses she saw. Each one was nestled in a lush tangle

of tropical foliage, and she caught sight of the sensuous blooms of hibiscus, morning glory and oleander.

The pastel washes of the coloured walls—pinks, mauves, creamy yellows—would have looked ridiculous against an English landscape but here they were just right, offset by the sloping white roofs which for some reason had corrugated ridges all over them like hills contour-ploughed for farming.

Soon they approached the island's southern shore and began to see the resort hotels and clubs that brought so many tourists to the island. With names like Blue Horizons and the Coral Beach and Tennis Club, they promised a tropical paradise which, in today's glorious weather, was fully delivered.

Then they began to pass an open park on their left, with hiking trails that led past rocky bluffs and seagrass-covered sandhills. A few minutes later, Anthony turned off down a winding and rather steep road that led towards the sea.

He parked near a large beach kiosk that contained dressing-room facilities as well as selling food and Jennie dismounted from the bike, her legs feeling a little stiff after the ride. She pulled off her safety helmet and shook out her hair in time to hear Anthony say, 'You started to relax there after a while.'

'Wasn't I relaxed at first?'

'No! Stiff as a board!'

'Well, it was a new experience,' she replied rather haughtily, too aware of the real reason for her initial stiffness. His fault!

He chuckled, then said repentantly, 'Teasing. Sorry.'

They headed for the beach. Having got away reasonably early and wasted no time getting lost *en route*, they had arrived before the crowds who would no doubt turn up as the day progressed. Jennie gasped and exclaimed at the sight of the ocean. It really was the most jewel-like aquamarine, shading to a rich, pure midnight-blue further out. The pink sand was the thing she had heard of, and it *was* pink, too, she found, unable to resist bending down to pick up a handful of the stuff.

Made largely of coral and shell, pounded by the sea into tiny fragments over the course of thousands of years, it was silky-fine as it slipped through her fingers, but its subtle pink hue was drowned by the more vibrant sea-tones so close by, and she couldn't wait to feel the salt water against her skin.

'Ready to swim?' Anthony asked beside her, obviously just as eager.

'Yes, please!'

Wearing white sandals and a brightly flowered sun-dress, Jennie took only a moment to slip out of these to reveal the bathing suit she had put on beneath her dress before leaving the ship. It was a dark royal purple, in audacious contrast to her bright hair, and was cut along classic one-piece lines, with accents in black piping and a rather low, curved dip in the back. She was ready for the water before Anthony had even finished pulling off his white leather running shoes and matching athletic socks.

Ready? He didn't think so. 'Don't forget your block-out cream. We're a lot closer to the equator than you're used to.'

Jennie was relieved at the reminder. . .and not just because she wanted to protect her skin. It meant she could dive into her beach-bag in search of the plastic bottle, absorb herself in carefully covering all vulner-able areas with cream, and only be half aware of the sight of Anthony Gray. His dorsal muscles rippled as he undid the top two buttons of his shirt and pulled it impatiently over his head, tousling that dark hair, then he reached to unzip those well-fitting jeans to reveal an equally close-fitting pair of black swimming-shorts.

Ridiculous! Why was she suddenly aware of him like this? It was all the fault of that idiotic scooter, which wasn't exactly a romantic mode of transport with its small, puttering motor and unflattering safety helmets. And now, to make matters worse, he had taken the bottle of block-out cream from her hand.

'You're bound to miss some spots on that bare back of yours. Here. . .' Without waiting for consent or refusal he squirted a cool pool of white cream into his palm and began to dab it on, using firm circular movements to cover every inch of skin.

Knowing that she had more than a few freckles on her back — and never having been too pleased at the fact — Jennie mentally poured cold water over the whole episode, and over her reaction to that scooter ride. Both events. . .could they even be called events?. . .had come about through sheer practical necessity. The fact that they had both made her aware of his masculinity and her own very female response to it only went to prove how horribly vulnerable she still was inside.

Somehow, this realisation had the desired effect, and she was able to return the favour and apply *his* block-out cream all over *his* back without thinking about it at all.

'Done? Good!' he said after a minute, sounding relieved, and suddenly they were both racing for the water as if this were a desert oasis and they were dying of thirst.

It was fabulous. There was only the slightest swell, so the waves built and broke gently and creamily on to the shore. The water temperature was perfect — cold enough to be utterly refreshing but without the sort of chill that caused Jennie's head muscles to tighten and ache in protest when she plunged into the waters off an English beach.

'The colour!' she called in delight to Anthony, who was as energetic and agile as a porpoise in the water.

'Yes! Like swimming in one of those ridiculous tropical cocktails, isn't it? A Blue Moon, no, *Lagoon*, or. . .'

'Turquoise Delight?' she improvised.

'How about Lapis l'Azur?' was his suggestion.

'Or — um — Opal Omniscience.'

'*What*?'

'Omniscience. It means all-knowing, doesn't it? People always think they know everything when they've had too many exotic liqueurs. They become embarrassingly wise, and ramble on and on. . .'

'True, but on the other hand, have you ever tried a Jade Fade?'

'No, but I'd love to. Why Fade?'

'As in tropical sunset. The light fading, you see.'

'That's terrible!'

'I know. No one would ever employ us to create an advertising campaign for Caribbean rum, would they?'

Altogether very silly. Probably the silliest conversation Jennie had had in months. And somehow it made her spirits feel very light. Turning away to hide the bubbling giggle of laughter that he couldn't possibly believe was caused by their inept punning, she dived once more into the water and swam until she was breathless just for the sheer joy of it.

She was thoroughly sated and more than a little water-logged by the time they both emerged from the ocean half an hour later.

'Want a walk along the hiking trail with lunch along the way?' Anthony suggested.

'Yes, please!'

They buffed the salty water from their bodies with towels and dressed again, then she picked up her beach-bag while he swung on to his shoulders the small nylon day-pack that had been strapped to the scooter's rear carrier. It was a delightful walk, although neither felt the need for much conversation. At Stonehole Bay they created a picnic spot in the shade of a rocky outcrop and had the rhythmic whisper of the sea as background music while they ate. Anthony produced bread rolls, cheese, cold meats and salads—a bounty that was left over from yesterday's lavish buffet lunch on the ship.

It was hot and bright on the beach now, and even these small, less accessible coves were well-occupied by swimmers and sunbathers, most in the unmistakable clothing of tourists.

'Want to see some more of the island this afternoon, or stay on the beach?' the doctor queried lazily, after the lunch remains had been packed away.

'Our shade is disappearing,' Jennie observed. 'I don't want to get caught like that Canadian patient of ours yesterday.'

'No, indeed!'

'So perhaps if we walk back, have another dip and brave that awful scooter again?'

'Awful? You didn't like it?'

What a thoughtless adjective! And how could she explain? Quickly she said, 'Yes, I *did* like it actually, once I got used to it. At first I wasn't too sure, I admit. But it's obviously a marvellous way to see the island, so. . .'

'Hmm.' He was hesitant and she knew she hadn't fully convinced him. Her own fault and further protestations would only make things worse. So she said brightly, 'But first I need that second swim.'

They walked quickly back to Horseshoe Beach, not stopping to look at tidal rock pools or unfamiliar sandhill plant life as they had done before lunch. Arriving on the dazzling sand once more, Jennie exclaimed a little breathlessly, 'Whew! That sun is more intense than I'm used to.'

'Definitely. But fortunately you've the sense to realise it. Some people don't.'

Hearing the sudden edge to his tone, she followed the direction of his gaze and saw a man flung face down on his towel on the beach, his back, a painful lobster-pink, fully exposed to the early afternoon rays.

'I don't believe it!' she breathed. 'That's not our Canadian friend, is it? Steve Waxman. . .'

'It is. A slow learner, evidently. And it looks as if he's asleep.' Anthony Gray's voice was steelier than ever.

'We don't know how long he's been here,' she pointed out. 'He may just have come out of the water and decided to take a minute to dry off.'

'No. His hair is quite dry, and look. . .that last wave almost caught the edge of his towel. The tide is coming in, and he wouldn't have laid himself out right within its reach.'

'That's true. But we had our camp just near this spot, didn't we? He wasn't here then, so. . .'

'We've been away for well over an hour. Closer to two. And ten minutes is too much for Mr Waxman today. Look, he'll hate me for it but I'm going to wake him up. I'll feel like a lecturing prig, but. . .' He swore capably under his breath. 'Some people are so damned *stupid*! You wait here. Or, better yet, start your dip. Don't get involved.'

'But. . .'

'Two of us standing there is only going to antagonise him more.'

'Antagonise! He should be grateful!'

'If I'm any judge of character, he'll be the opposite.'

Anthony Gray evidently *was* quite a judge of character. Not liking to abandon him entirely to what might be an unpleasant scene, Jennie took her time in laying out her towel and removing sun-hat, dress and sandals. She touched up her block-out cream on face, shoulders and throat as well, and as she did so she could watch the angry scene that flared quickly between the two men, although she could catch only a few of the outspoken words that carried above the insistent wash of the sea.

Anthony was back only a minute or two later. 'What happened?' she asked him unnecessarily.

'Told me to mind my own business.'

'It *is* your business!'

'Not in his opinion.'

'Had he been there long?'

'Since before noon, he admits.'

'But not drinking, surely, after yesterday. . .'

'You mustn't credit others with your sort of good sense, Jennie. Yes, he *has* been drinking, and British beer, too, which is usually twice as strong as the North American variety.'

'Sun-block cream?' she queried tersely. 'I did give him a sample of factor fifteen yesterday.'

'He's using factor three. Scarcely worth a thing with skin already fried like his. He seems obsessed with going back to his office tanned.'

'He'll be going back in gauze bandages at this rate.'

'Oh, no,' Anthony answered sarcastically. 'Didn't you know? This is the way to do it. All you have to do is take a very hot shower at the end of the day and put on several coatings of after-sun lotion, and in a day or two you'll have a perfect dark tan, and no ill-effects at all.'

'*What*?'

'His theory. If I hadn't seen his beer I'd say he'd been drinking some of your Opal Omniscience.'

She had to laugh at this, and they said no more about

the too eager tanner. They had no authority here on the beach, and if their erstwhile patient refused to take well-meant medical advice there was nothing they could do about it. But their swim this time was definitely not as much fun, although they stayed in for another full half-hour. Mr Waxman had moved his towel out of the reach of the incoming tide after his altercation with Anthony, and was still flung out on it when they emerged.

'Let's not towel off thoroughly now,' Anthony suggested, ignoring the man. 'There are fresh-water showers at the beach kiosk. If you still want a scooter ramble. . .'

'Shower first? Good idea. I brought underclothing.'

'Yes, we'll both feel much less sticky and gritty.'

Gathering their things quickly, and exchanging one last silent, helpless glance as they walked past their frying and dehydrating patient, they set off down the beach. But it was only a minute or two later that they were overtaken by flying footsteps and an older American hailed them breathlessly. 'Are you the doctor and nurse from our ship? The *Leeward*?'

'Yes, we are,' Anthony answered for them both.

'There's a guy back there, very burned. He's asking for you. He looks pretty ill. Can barely speak.'

Knowing just what the problem was, they were actually relieved to be able to turn back and deal with it at last.

CHAPTER FOUR

'YOUR afternoon was ruined,' Anthony Gray said to Jennie an hour and a half later when they finally emerged from the ship's hospital, leaving Steve Waxman in Sister Balasingham's charge.

'Yours, too,' she pointed out to him.

'I've seen Bermuda before.'

Both were still in their swimming costumes, with dress or jeans flung hastily on top of sandy, salty skin so that, with time to take stock now, they felt itchy and uncomfortable from salt-stiffened hair to beach-toughened toes.

The tan-obsessed Canadian had been suffering from heatstroke, and it could have been very serious. When they had reached him, he was clearly dizzy, weak and nauseous. Reaching for his pulse and touching his skin in several other places, Anthony had said urgently, 'He's not sweating and his pulse is far too fast. He's febrile, too, and if his temperature rises any further we may be too late.'

Jennie had raced for the water without waiting another moment, intending to saturate their towels with cooling sea-water, but before she could lift the heavy, dripping cloths from the waves Anthony was beside her, carrying the solidly built man as if he were merely a child. The doctor had laid their patient in the shallow water and told Jennie, 'Cover him with those towels. We've got to cool him before we even try to get him back to the ship. . .or to the hospital if it looks too bad. There's a first-aid kit in the side-pocket of that day-pack. Bring aspirin and a thermometer.'

As he spoke, he was massaging the man, not caring that he might be chafing skin already raw with sunburn. Steve Waxman's life was in danger, and he seemed to be in a stupor now, in no condition to object to some superficial pain. The massage was a vital element in circulating the cooling blood near the surface of his body more quickly to vital centres such as the heart and brain.

Jennie had returned quickly with the aspirin and the remains of the juice she and Anthony had drunk at lunchtime. She had given the drug clumsily as their patient was unable to understand that she needed him to swallow, but at last it had been successfully downed. The man from the ship who had alerted them to the Canadian's illness had found someone with a large beach umbrella and a concerned group of onlookers had helped to erect it, its pointed pole awash with sea-water, so that it shaded both the patient and the doctor and nurse who were working over him.

'Is there anything else we can do?' the *Leeward* passenger asked.

'Yes. Call an ambulance.'

While they were waiting — and they knew it would take a while for an ambulance to be alerted and to reach them, since they were at the far end of the beach — Anthony turned Steve Waxman face down, pillowing his head to one side against his own towel while he re-soaked and draped the other towels over the rest of the inert body. To get an accurate reading of internal body temperature, he was forced to use the thermometer rectally, taking a new reading every five minutes to chart the gradual return to near normal. The readings had started at a hundred and eight degrees, but had come down to a hundred and one by the time the ambulance arrived.

'I want to go with him, Jennie. Can you manage that scooter?'

'I think so. . .yes! Of course I can! Just give me the keys.'

'To King Edward Memorial?' the ambulance officers wanted to know.

'To the *Leeward*. We have everything that's needed there to treat this, and I think we got to him in time to prevent permanent damage.'

'To the *Leeward*, then.'

The patient was carried by stretcher along the beach, still draped in towels that had now been wrung dry, as the body would continue to cool on its own and there was now, paradoxically, a danger that the man's temperature might fall too low. All this time, Anthony continued his vigorous massaging, and before the ambulance doors closed Jennie could see him beginning it again, this time to help counter the constriction of blood vessels produced by the cold as well as to continue to try and bring cooler blood to the brain.

Tense about the patient's condition and nervous about the scooter, Jennie was much slower than the ambulance in reaching the ship. She made a rather wobbly stop in a scooter parking space, not knowing if it was reserved for anyone special and not having time to care. In the ship's hospital, Anthony had already begun more sophisticated treatment of Steve Waxman's condition, helped by Tilly, whom he had paged as soon as he arrived. An IV line had been set up, delivering a rapid dose of both fluids and medication, and now all they could do was wait and watch. The Canadian seemed more aware of his surroundings now, but was not yet able to speak coherently.

'He'll recover,' was the senior doctor's terse aside to Jennie and Tilly, 'but I doubt that his temperature control mechanisms will function normally for some time, perhaps for years, and he won't be able to tolerate hot weather at all. I hope he has the sense to realise after this that he has literally had a brush with death. Death, not blistered skin and a hangover the next day!'

Finally, they were able to leave, with Hector alerted to what had happened and both he and Tilly made fully conversant with the ongoing observtions that had to be made and warning signs to watch for. Anthony growled with a frown. 'Perhaps I should stay. . .'

But Hector pointed out with a touch of asperity, 'I'm a doctor, too, remember? And I'm the one on duty. What more could you do that I can't?'

'True,' Anthony said. 'So why do I feel guilty about leaving? Because this whole thing is the man's own damn fault, I suppose, and I can't quite feel the professional sympathy that I should.'

'Professional sympathy? Hey. . .' Hector spread his hands and smiled disarmingly '. . .I can do that too!' A shared laugh improved moods all round.

Walking down the corridor now, Jennie couldn't wait for a long shower and shampoo. Those fresh, massaging needles of water, that snake-like hose that she could unhook and play all over her body. . . The hungry reverie was interrupted by the senior doctor. 'Look, we have that scooter for the rest of the day, and it's only four o'clock. Why not go for a spin to the far end of the island and have dinner? I'd like some more time away from the ship now that the drama is all over, and I'm sure you would too.'

'Not until I've had a shower!'

'Good heavens, no!' The fervency of his response told her that he had been thinking of it with equal longing, and she laughed. 'Make it an hour, then, shall we?' he suggested. 'Give yourself plenty of time to dress.'

'Don't expect anything too glamorous.'

'Please! It's a scooter, remember, not a stretch limousine, and we won't go anywhere too formal.' They reached her cabin. 'Oh, and Jennie. . .?'

'Yes?'

'Have two or three long glasses of water. We didn't have a lot of fruit juice at lunch and I don't want to have to hook you up to that IV line as well.'

'Certainly not!'

They parted company, and as she undressed and took the first of the drinks he had prescribed she could hear water running very faintly through her own bathroom wall. So it was his cabin next door! She had suspected as much, but hadn't been sure, as so far they had not arrived at or left their cabins at the same time.

There was something a little disturbing about knowing that they were separated by so little. . . No. How silly! Now that she had turned on her own taps, she couldn't hear a thing from next door, and no doubt after this afternoon they might come and go for days more without encountering one another. Hector's cabin, she already knew, was the next one along from Anthony's. *That* was the one she ought to feel self-conscious about, since there was a strong likelihood that it wouldn't just be Hector that she would see emerging from it at odd hours over the coming weeks. . .

'Come on, Jennie!' she scolded herself aloud. 'Just enjoy your shower, would you, girl, and stop worrying yourself over nothing?'

The scolding had its effect, and after Anthony Gray's prescribed hour she was refreshed and very ready for that scooter again. She had chosen navy blue silk trousers that were loose and full around her thighs before gathering in to an elastic cuff at each ankle. Teamed with a simple cream blouse and matching lightweight navy silk evening jacket, the outfit ought to be comfortable for their exploratory ride, yet dressy enough for any restaurant.

Anthony must think so, anyway, if she was correctly reading the brief nod he gave at the sight of her. Actually, she was a little disappointed that he didn't say more. One thing about Ralph. . .he had always commented on her appearance, usually with judicious approval, occasionally with a stiff, tight note that told her she hadn't chosen quite the right thing this time.

Then she brought herself up short, and not for the first time today. There was no reason whatsoever to be comparing Anthony Gray with Ralph Caine, no matter who was flattered by such comparisons!

'Where are we going?' she asked Anthony quickly.

'West, unless you have a different preference.'

'No, I'm in your hands on this.'

'Then I thought we'd take the Harbour Road and then the Middle Road all the way out to the Royal Naval Dockyard. Just a quick look there, and back to Somerset for dinner overlooking the water. There's an old stone inn I know of. . .'

'Seafood?' she asked hopefully.

'Of course!'

The ride was glorious. They were both confident enough together on the small machine now to take each bend or corner smoothly, and Jennie found that she only needed to hold the senior doctor very lightly around the waist in order to be confident of her balance. The speed limit on Bermuda's narrow, winding roads was low and Anthony made no attempt to exceed it.

Every vista that Jennie glimpsed was tantalising, whether it was of that ridiculously luminescent aquamarine ocean bobbing with boats, or of some tranquil, pastel-hued old house, dating from farming and seafaring days, with wide verandas and a surrounding of palms and tropical figs.

'Not cold?' Anthony threw back at her above the high-pitched puttering of the motor as they left the harbourside road.

'Not at all.'

'Bored?'

'*Bored*? You're joking!'

The ride seemed all too short. They spent half an hour wandering around the old stone buildings of the Royal Naval Dockyard, which was now a complex of shops, restaurants and a maritime museum, and Jennie had to tear herself away, inwardly promising a day trip here by ferry some time in the future.

'I made a booking at the restaurant,' Anthony said, as Jennie lingered over some locally made jewellery.

'I know. I'm sorry.'

'We can skip it if you like.'

'No!' She faced him for a moment. 'Please don't make it seem as if the evening is just for me! *Is* it? Would you like to stay on here. . .or go?'

He laughed. 'We're both being far too polite about this, aren't we?'

Briefly, their glances met with an awareness that touched at Jennie's core and confused her. What was 'this'? She had thought she knew. Anthony Gray was courteously stepping in to show his new nurse the island, nothing more. Now. . . Having guessed that in some private way he was as vulnerable and questing as she was, she wondered, was this evening safe? For the first time since yesterday's fiasco with Hector, she regretted the absence of the shallower junior doctor.

Choosing honesty as the best response to Anthony, she said quickly, 'Lunch seems a long time ago and I haven't eaten decent seafood in months.'

'Good decision.'

Another exhilarating ride brought them to the old stone inn that overlooked an open bay in Somerset.

The place was busy already, and when Anthony gave his name the young man frowned over the reservations book then grew flustered. 'I'm sorry. . .you were ten minutes late. I. . . I seem to have given your table to someone else.'

Another meaningful glance was exchanged between Jennie and Anthony, this time one of frank, hungry disappointment.

'If you could wait half an hour?' came an anguished plea.

For a moment, the doctor's face tightened with impatience and anger, reminding Jennie of the way she had first seen him four days ago — only four days! — with that terrible migraine headache. Then he sighed and his face relaxed again. 'We *were* late.'

'My fault,' murmured Jennie.

'Yes, we can wait half an hour,' he told the anxious young man.

'Possibly less,' the latter came in quickly. 'There is a perfect table by the windows. The couple have finished their main course. . .'

'It's all right. We'll have a drink at the bar, shall we, Jennie? I thought you might fancy an Opal Omniscience.'

She twisted her mouth at him and said drily, 'I was thinking more of your suggestion. Don't they do a good Jade Fade here?'

Leaving a bewildered junior *maître d'hotel* behind them, they headed towards the bar.

'We're going to have to stop having these silly conversations about drinks!'

'We are. . .'

'What will you really have, Jennie?' Anthony asked her as they settled in to a small booth at the quietest end of the crowded room.

'Actually, I *do* fancy something silly and tropical, but I can't think what.'

'Piña colada? Margarita?' He reeled off several more exotic names.

'Heavens! Were you a barman in a former life?'

Laughingly, he gestured at a blackboard behind her. 'I'm cheating. Those are all today's cocktail specials.'

'And I was so impressed!'

'How about a pink gin?'

'Never had one.'

'Neither have I.'

'But it sounds just right.'

It *was* just right, too, very light and refreshing, and, Jennie suspected, a lot stronger than it seemed. When the cocktail waitress returned and suggested another, she shook her head and so did Anthony.

'We've been here half an hour,' he said.

'That long?' Jennie blurted in surprise.

They had been talking about Bermuda — the significance of its onions, the reason its houses all had such funny roofs. This was to catch water, Jennie had discovered, as the island depended on this run-off for its entire supply. . . And somehow they had been here for half an hour.

Not long enough, though, it seemed. The flustered junior *maître d'hotel* who had greeted them before was again obliged to apologise. 'They ordered dessert. Another fifteen minutes, sir. . . And we hope you will accept a bottle of wine on the house.'

'Another drink?' Anthony murmured to Jennie. 'Or shall we give up on this disastrous establishment and try somewhere else?'

His tone had tightened. Jennie laid an impulsive hand on his arm, feeling a pale Swiss cotton shirt very fine and smooth beneath her fingertips. 'No sense getting angry.'

'I thought you were the one with the temper.'

'Not over things like this.'

'No. You're right, of course. I——' He stopped abruptly, and she could see that now he was angry with himself. Equally unproductive.

'Can we go for a walk outside?' she came in quickly. 'The smells in here are just too savoury and appetising when we won't be eating for another half an hour.'

'Excellent idea!' His face relaxed at once and Jennie took her hand quickly away. 'There's a little wharf just a few minutes' walk away, and a marina,' he suggested. 'I love the sound of nautical ropes hitting aluminium masts in the evening breeze.'

'Yes, and the lap of water on hulls.'

'And sometimes a small yacht heading out in the darkness under low power. Just a light and a puttering motor moving across the water.'

They were silent for a while after this, walking down a darkened street until they could hear just the sounds that each had described. There was no moving yacht tonight, but light from houses on the opposite side of the bay stretched yellow and white fingers across the blackly shimmering water.

It was like the other night when they had stood together watching the *Leeward* plough its powerful way forward, and it created the same mood of dangerous intimacy between them.

Anthony said, 'Thanks for making me see reason back there. You were right. So much better to shrug our shoulders and enjoy ourselves anyway. Sometimes I don't know when to turn and fight and when to run away.'

'Was this running away?' she asked softly.

'This? No, I suppose it wasn't. I was thinking more generally. I suppose I haven't quite made up my mind yet. Is running away, when it comes to the larger issues of life, ever the right thing to do?'

'Sometimes it's the *only* thing to do,' she answered him at once.

'Speaking from experience?' It was a lazy query, but the intention behind it was very serious.

'You mean, for me, was coming to work on the *Leeward* running away?'

'Yes.'

'Of course it was!'

'Of course?'

'Isn't nearly everyone who works on this ship running away? Or at least taking time off from the real course of their lives?'

'You're a fast learner.'

She went on, 'The social directors, the boutique staff, even the waiters. They're all here to make extra money to send home or to spend on their educations, or they wanted a year or two of travel and adventure before settling down to marriage or a career. Or they have some problem at home that just seemed too hard to get through without some time and distance. Why should it be different for us?'

'Why indeed?'

Had she gone too far? That response of his was very laconic and bland. . . Then she realised that he was thinking. 'You sound very confident,' he said.

'More confident than I sometimes feel,' she admitted.

'And how will you know when it's time to go back?'

'Be fair, Dr Gray! I've only been here for four days!'

He laughed, and Jennie was glad. They had both been straying into deep waters. A little lightness would surely break the mood. Somehow, it didn't, though. Instead, she found that he was studying her, and there was something so hypnotic about that serious, grey-

eyed gaze above the full upper lip and straight nose
that her own glance was drawn to it and held there.

She was aware, all at once, of how close they were
standing — so close that she could feel his warmth and
could have reached up to wind her arms around his
neck without taking another step. His lips were slightly
parted, emphasising their firm shape and revealing a
glint of white teeth inside the darkened space of his
mouth. Dark hair blew into small, ruffled wings at his
temples, making her fingers suddenly itch to caress
them back into place.

His compact waist was a few inches higher than her
own, and her neatly rounded breasts would have
pressed against his ribcage with its webbing of muscle
had she leaned just a few inches closer. She wanted to
do so, and was certain that he felt the same, certain
that he was going to kiss her. She was so certain of it,
in fact, that her own lips parted and her eyes began to
drift shut so that she saw him only through a blurred
haze of lashes.

For a moment, time stood still. They both swayed
forward and she felt his lips brush hers with a whisper
of touch. His cotton shirt grazed the firm twin mounds
that rose and fell with her rapid breathing beneath the
silky cream blouse.

Then, a moment later, it was over. He drew a
shuddering sigh of breath and said quickly, 'They'll give
away our table again if we don't hurry.'

His warm palm came to make a delicate tracery of
touch along her jawline, leaving a tingling like fire, then
somehow they were both walking back up the dark
road towards the beckoning lights and sizzling aromas
of the old stone inn.

Between them now there was silence, broken only by
the rhythm of their determined footsteps on the stone
pavement. Jennie didn't have time to wonder what he

was thinking or feeling. She was consumed with her own whirling emotions—confusion, regret, longing. Yes, she still longed for his touch, longed to reach out even now and consummate the moment, and as she began to relax a little more and breathe normally— instead of at that rapid, heart-thumping pace that his touch had triggered—she was certain that he felt the same.

We should never have talked about running away, she thought feverishly. Never even let ourselves hint to each other that there might be something in our lives that we share. I didn't leave England to. . . I feel as if I've been wrecked on a desert island with him, and he and I are the only ones who know it.

This very disturbing sensation did not go away. They were ushered to their table at last and presented with a perfectly chilled bottle of very decent Californian wine. Soon, sizzling platters of seafood were set before them and appetites that had seemed urgent only minutes before—but were now strangely weak and acquiescent—could at last be satisfied.

Jennie's chest was tight and she was almost trembling. The wine seemed like a refuge, something that might steady her, and she took generous sips of it over the course of fifteen minutes before realising that it was only making her light-headed and less in control than before.

His eyes seemed darker tonight, pools of cool stormy grey. No, not cool at all, and certainly not stormy. Warm. Very warm and liquid and deep. Or was it only the mellow golden light of the restaurant that made them seem that way? His smile was slow and full, his voice low and caressing.

'Enjoying the lobster?'

'Mmm, perfect. And how are your prawns?'

'Marvellous.'

'Had you been here before?'

'Just for a drink, but I'd been told the food was good.'

'Your informant was right.'

'We'll have to come again and try all those other dishes on the menu that almost tempted us.'

'Nice to know that we'll be back in Bermuda again next week.'

There was nothing of great substance to their conversation. It was as if they were each instinctively steering away from anything that might require too much personal revelation. There had already been enough of *that* this evening for two people whose main connection to each other was that they had stories they wanted to remain untold.

Was it really their main connection? It didn't seem that way at the moment. Her new and dramatic physical awareness of the man opposite created what Jennie — even swimming in food and wine and light as she was — recognised as a dangerous illusion of greater closeness.

It was getting late, and by wordless agreement they did not linger over the meal, deciding against dessert and coffee. Holding him once again as she sat behind him on the impertinent little bike, Jennie found it incredibly difficult to keep herself from nuzzling her face — even in its less than romantic helmet! — against his warm back and losing herself in the rhythmic sensation of his chest expanding and falling with his steady breathing.

The result was that this time their ride together was stiff and awkward, and the small machine seemed to jerk and pull on the bends instead of flowing smoothly through them.

'Tired?' he asked laconically as they got off the scooter for the last time.

'I must be,' she admitted. 'I should be. I don't feel it, but. . .'

The scooter-rental garage seemed to be deserted at this hour. 'We'll walk back, shall we?' he suggested. 'It's not far. I'll drop back here in the morning to return the key and pick up the deposit.'

'Mmm-hmm.'

They began walking together along the wharf side of Front Street. All the souvenir shops on the opposite side were closed now, and just a few groups of people strolled back from nearby restaurants or went into pubs for a late drink. Ahead of them loomed the *Leeward*, quiet although its upper decks and many of its cabin windows were lit.

Coming alongside the bows, Jennie instinctively slowed and stopped to look at the huge vessel against the backdrop of dark harbour water that she could see just beyond the prow. Anthony stopped too, and suddenly the sensual tension and connection that had been so strong between them all evening sighed effortlessly into a kiss that seemed quite inevitable.

His fingers threaded through her rich red hair, making her scalp tingle and thrill, then they slid downwards to caress the nape of her neck. His lips—that full, sensuous upper curve and the finer one beneath— were gently parted as they closed over hers, softly at first then with increasing demand. Jennie's response was like a tide, strong, steady and unquestioning.

His cheeks were warm, his lips travelled down to her throat, then, as he gave a shuddering sigh, returned to her mouth again to taste her hungrily. Their noses bumped and nudged together and her hands searched his body for more delicious places to touch and linger at. The strong hollow of the small of his back, the muscled wall of his chest, the ropy curves of strength at his shoulders. . .

When it ended, as it had to, they were both breathless and trembling, and their walk through Customs and back to the *Leeward* was full of unspoken feelings. As they reached her cabin door, Jennie knew that he would kiss her again, and she wanted it so badly that it frightened her.

This time the joy of mouth touching mouth was even more abandoned and passionate. Anthony gave himself to their kiss completely. Letting her eyes drift briefly open, Jennie saw the two black crescents of his lashes resting against the high hollows at the top of his cheekbones, making a delicious contrast of dark and pale.

His arms wrapped around her, so warm and firm that if they had been drowning together in an inky sea the touch of those arms would have kept her afloat for hours. At last, when she was in danger of forgetting everything but the moment, he groaned and released her, slowly and reluctantly. 'Go to bed, Jennie. Sleep it off.'

'Sleep. . .?'

'We must have drunk too much of that Californian wine. Or had too much sun and sea at the beach today. Sleep it off,' he repeated more firmly, as much an order to himself as to her, it seemed.

Fumbling for her flat plastic key-card, Jennie at first wanted to protest. It wasn't the wine. It wasn't the swimming or the caress of the sun. Those things were hours ago, and the ride home from the restaurant had cleared her head of any wine. Then she realised what he was saying. . .what he was asking of her and why, and she knew that he was right.

Neither of them needed or wanted this complication in their lives. For Jennie, the self-doubt that Ralph had raised in her was still far too fresh and strong. For Anthony. . . Well, she didn't know, but there was something. Some battle he was fighting, some quest he was on. Ironically, the intuition that each had about the other's life in England was the thing that had to keep them apart, as well as the thing — not the wine, not the beach — that had brought them so dangerously close tonight.

'Yes,' she agreed quickly in a fervent whisper. 'It was the wine. We probably won't even remember it in the morning.'

'Sensible.'

'We're both very sensible, aren't we?'

'I hope so,' he murmured.

The key clicked in the lock and she fell into the darkened cabin, closing the door behind her. While she still stood there, her eyes adjusting to the dimness, she heard his own door open and shut, followed by silence.

Over towards the porthole, Tilly's bed contained a humped, motionless shape, giving off the light, peaceful sound of sleepy breathing. Hector must be with Steve Waxman for the moment, but no doubt Tilly would take over at some point during the night, as no patient was ever left alone in the small hospital. Moving quietly and cautiously, Jennie undressed in the darkness, slipping into a cream cotton nightdress and taking five minutes in the bathroom to freshen herself for the night. Very soon, she was in bed.

During her own night preparations she had not heard any sounds from Anthony's cabin next door, but now she *did* hear something, and it was not what she might have expected at all. Music. The faint, air-filled sound of a reed flute playing some slow, haunting melody. Not a radio or a cassette tape. Definitely not the American television shows that were beamed by satellite to every cabin on the ship. Anthony was playing. Just loudly enough to be audible. Just softly enough to be incredibly beautiful and soothing.

Having expected to lie awake for hours reliving his kiss — regretting it, wanting more of it — Jennie found instead that her limbs were relaxing and her eyes were growing sticky and heavy with sleep. In just a few minutes she had drifted away, floating on the sweet sound of Anthony Gray's flute.

CHAPTER FIVE

JENNIE awoke late the next morning to the dull sound of the ship's engines and a faint feeling of motion. Scrambling quickly from the covers, she opened the crimson curtains and looked out of the round port-hole. No land in sight on this side.

They had left the harbour at Hamilton and were making the short trip around to St George's, where the *Leeward* would remain until tomorrow afternoon, before heading back to New York. Tilly's bed was empty and neatly made.

I must have slept like a log all night, Jennie realised blankly.

She felt refreshed and not in the least bit heavy-headed as she had half expected to. So much for the effects of the wine that she and Anthony had so carefully agreed upon last night.

Anthony. . .! She was supposed to be in the surgery with him at ten o'clock this morning. What was the time now? Only a little after nine, she saw with relief as she found the watch beside her bed. Time to shower and dress and eat a proper breakfast before facing. . . what? She had no reason to feel apprehensive about the morning, she told herself firmly. Any potential problem between them — embarrassment, regret — had surely been nipped in the bud by his insistence on blaming the wine.

'Clever man!' she said aloud to the mirror as she dressed. 'Thank goodness for that!'

He had just opened the surgery when she arrived

there three-quarters of an hour later, and his greeting was cheerful. 'Sleep well?'

'Very, thanks.'

'It's the sea air.'

'I expect so.' She forced herself to lock glances with him, willing her blue-eyed gaze to remain steady. It did, and so did his, then both looked away.

Another hurdle successfully cleared. She had been afraid that both of them would be too inclined to stare blankly into the middle distance or furtively at their shoes, with uncomfortable awareness flowing between them like some sticky, smelly glue.

'What sort of patients are we likely to see this morning?' she asked brightly now.

'Don't know. Could be quiet,' he answered with equal good humour as he went to open up his surgery-cum-office. 'No "road rash" from scooter rides. Hardly time for anyone to get seasick before we dock again, which should be any minute. I dropped in here earlier this morning, and Hector and I decided to discharge Steve Waxman at his own request. We would have kept him longer, but even now he's so belligerent about the whole thing. He had a good night, though, his vital signs are all back to normal and he's coming back this afternoon to have those burns dressed. I'll look in on his cabin directly after surgery hours this morning, too.'

'He's been lucky, then, really.'

'Indeed! And I told him so in no uncertain terms. Made it quite clear that any kind of exposure to sun and heat, especially combined with exertion or alcohol, was out of the question, possibly for years. I don't think he's fully taken it in yet, and I've told him I want to see him at both morning and evening surgery hours until the end of the cruise. After that, I'm going to send a copy of his case-file to his own GP at home and insist that he make an appointment for a full check-up as soon as possible.'

Jennie was disturbed to find herself hoping it *would* be a quiet morning as Anthony had predicted. She liked the idea of being alone with him here, not speaking much, making coffee later on. Perhaps she would ask him about that flute music she had heard from his cabin last night. There would be other things to talk about, too. It had a warm, peaceful feeling. . .too much so! Perhaps last night's kiss had been even more dangerous than she realised. . .

And in the end it wasn't a quiet morning at all. Their patient of the other day, Chester Brady, returned to them complaining of further chest pain. He was overweight, a smoker, pale, sweaty and frightened, and he *hadn't* fully taken Dr Gray's advice to rest and avoid the over-indulgence in food that was so easy on these cruises.

'He had the soup and salad and fish for dinner last night, just as you suggested,' his wife assured the medical pair while Dr Gray was quietly and efficiently examining him and noting the results of the blood-pressure and pulse readings that Jennie had taken. 'No dessert at all, but then. . .' She looked timidly at her husband and he glared back, including Anthony and Jennie in the fierceness of his gaze.

'Damn fool of a thing, this cruise,' he rumbled. '"Relax in the sun", they said in the brochure. And then you, Doctor, telling me to take it easy. Nothing to do at all! What else is there to think about but food, with all those feasts being served at every hour of the day, and twenty-four-hour room service? Yes! I went up to the midnight buffet and I overate.'

'He had heartburn all night, Doctor.'

'Did you take anything for it?'

'I keep a bottle of that chalky stuff with me. Drink

the vile brew as if it were whisky, sometimes. I often have heartburn. That's nothing, is it?' he glared again. 'Perfectly normal in a man of my age.'

'If you mean is it part of any actual heart problem? Not as such,' Anthony answered. 'But it does mean your system is working too hard and it doesn't have to be "normal". Digestion isn't an easy process, you know. It takes a lot of energy and it draws quite a bit of blood from other parts of your body. You can do a lot to limit heartburn through what and how you eat.'

'You mean a diet?' Mr Brady queried suspiciously.

'Not necessarily.' Anthony stopped and glanced at Jennie. With his talk of indigestion, the patient had got them on to a side-track that was important but not urgent at this stage. Time to get back to the real issue. 'Now, your blood-pressure and pulse were not what they should be. I want to keep you in here for an hour or two and treat you for angina. Then, if you're still having any pain or other symptoms, I'm going to transfer you by ambulance to the coronary care unit at King Edward Memorial Hospital just outside Hamilton. We just don't have the equipment here fully to diagnose the problem, let alone treat it.'

'Take him to the hospital?' Mrs Brady came in, horrified. 'But. . .our cruise. You think it could be that serious? A real heart attack?'

'Damn fool of a cruise!' Chester Brady muttered belligerently again, as if it were Anthony and Jennie who had compelled him to board the *Leeward* and take a very luxurious cabin on the ninth deck.

'Surely you don't want to take any chances,' Anthony said gently. 'Once we put to sea again tomorrow afternoon, more sophisticated care is a day and a half away. The ship cannot turn around or change course for a medical emergency, and it doesn't have the facilities for medical evacuation by air.'

'Then you're saying he could still be in the hospital in Bermuda when we sail tomorrow?' Mrs Brady said.

'I hope not,' answered Anthony. 'But you may find that's for the best. I don't want to alarm you. . .'

'You *have* alarmed us, alarmed my wife, anyway,' Mr Brady growled ominously, pulling himself up from a slumped position on the doctor's examining table, then he stiffened and groaned as a spasm of pain seized him again.

Jennie had nitroglycerine tablets at the ready and Dr Gray took one and told Mr Brady to place it under his tongue. In a remarkably short time, the dark furrows on his brow cleared as the pain ebbed.

'That's a good sign,' Dr Gray told him.

Fifteen minutes later, the grumpy New Yorker was fully settled into his hospital bed with his wife determined to remain beside him.

'When will you decide about transferring him?' Jennie asked Anthony quietly as they returned to his surgery.

'I *have* decided,' the doctor returned. 'I'm going to do it. For medical reasons, partly. We really *don't* have the facilities here to find out if there's anything beyond that angina and heartburn. But I confess there's more to it than that. This patient looks to me like the type who might sue the hell out of this shipping company if anything more goes wrong, and unfortunately that has to be part of my brief these days—to see such an eventuality coming and do what I can to prevent it, which in this case means taking the most cautious route possible.'

Jennie made a wry face. 'And if there is a serious heart problem?'

'An air transfer from Bermuda to hospital in New York as soon as the doctors at KEMH think his condition is stable enough.'

'Hmm. . .'

'I expect that's what *will* happen, too. He's a prime candidate for heart problems, and I imagine his own doctor must have spoken to him in the past about risk factors. To no effect, it seems.'

Jennie left the surgery and was about to set herself up in the small dispensary, where she wanted to start work on the list of requisitions that was due to be made. Typically, it was a time-consuming procedure and she hoped that Tilly's explanation of the steps involved had stuck firmly enough in her mind. But as she opened the dispensary door she heard voices entering the waiting-room.

'I can feel it. . .' A panic-stricken woman.

'*Feel* it? Darling. . .' An equally frightened and very solicitous man.

'Yes. Warm. Tons of it. Just like the miscarriage. My shorts are soaked already. Look. Oh, David! If it's another one. . .'

A distressed husband and wife had entered and Jennie could see the widening stain of red in the seat of the woman's white canvas shorts. Coming quickly forward, she said at once, 'Take our second room here. Lie down and I'll get the doctor straight away. It's a first trimester bleed, is it?'

'Yes, and I've already had one miscarriage several months ago.'

'Let's get you settled.'

Jennie spread out an absorbent, plastic-shielded paper sheet on the bed in Ward Two and took a clean blue hospital gown from a storage cupboard. She could see from the stained shorts that the bleeding was heavy and fresh, and could only cross her fingers about its cause. If this *was* the beginning of a miscarriage, little could be done to prevent it now. 'Undress and put this on. Dr Gray will need to examine you. Any cramping?'

'No, none at all. That's good, isn't it?' the woman asked pleadingly.

'Yes, it usually is,' Jennie agreed cautiously, not wanting to raise hopes at his stage.

She had been expecting Anthony to appear without being summoned, having assumed he would hear the arrival of the couple and guess from their voice-tones that something was wrong, but evidently he *hadn't* heard, and when she knocked on his surgery door she found him completely absorbed in an article from the *British Medical Journal*.

'My friend Stephen Greer,' he said, lifting the journal and laying it down again. Jennie caught a glimpse of the black and white photo of an older and very distinguished-looking medical man. 'There's not a patient, is there?'

'Yes.'

He frowned. 'I didn't hear. What is it?'

'A first trimester bleed. Pretty heavy. No cramping. Nine weeks' gestation, one previous miscarriage,' she summarised briefly.

At once the preoccupation that Jennie had seen hovering over him dissipated like the last shreds of a morning fog at sea. 'Febrile?'

'I haven't checked yet. They seem pretty upset. I thought the quicker you examined her. . .'

'Right. I'm on my way.'

He washed his hands quickly but thoroughly and slipped them into thin surgical gloves as he left the surgery. Closing and locking it behind her — protocol was strict here — Jennie followed him, bringing equipment to measure blood-pressure and temperature. She replaced the stained paper sheet on the bed with a fresh one, then stood aside, patting the woman's arm in a gesture of reassurance. These next few minutes might be very hard ones for her.

Dr Gray went to work, slipping his hands beneath the blue gown and palpating the woman's abdomen before using a speculum and light to examine the condition of the cervix. 'There's a clot here,' he said. 'Is this the first you've passed?'

'No, I think there have been a couple more. I went to the bathroom in our cabin, and——'

'Any tissue? Stringy, greyish. . .'

'We know,' the husband came in quickly. 'Like last time. We didn't see any.'

'That's good,' Anthony reassured them. 'And there's no dilation of the cervix. That's good too. Your uterus is about the size it should be at this stage, and in fact the bleeding seems to be easing. Still no cramping?'

'No.'

'Jennie?'

'Blood-pressure, temperature and pulse all good.'

There was a small silence then Anthony took a pace backwards. 'Look,' he said gently. 'I don't want to make any promises at this stage. I'm pretty positive that you've still got a living baby in there. This bleeding. . . I don't want to say it's normal but it does happen to some women. There are a lot of new blood vessels in there and they have a lot of work to do. Sometimes one of them will break and this happens. When your obstetrician examines the placenta after your baby is born, he or she may find some scarring.'

'Is that something to worry about?' the husband came in anxiously.

'Not at all. Nature is generous that way. She gives you plenty of placenta is case some of it does get damaged.'

'Then you think. . .'

'There's only one way to be completely sure, and to set your mind at rest, and that's a foetal sonogram. Of course we don't have an ultrasound scanning machine

here on board, but I can arrange for you to go to the
hospital here in Bermuda and have one there. If you
want that reassurance. . .and I understand that of
course you probably do. . .'

'Yes, please!' said the woman fervently.

New hope after near despair had brightened her fair,
pretty features, but when Anthony left to phone the
hospital and arrange for both Mr Brady and the new
patient's treatment she burst into tears. 'I still can't
believe it. I *won't* believe it until the sonogram. What
will we be able to see, Sister McDougall?'

Jennie had to think hard for a moment. Obstetrics
wasn't her area. 'A heartbeat. A foetal sac. Some
movement of limbs, I think. I do know that at nine
weeks it's definite. There won't be any room for
ambiguity.'

The woman, Jessica Heilpern — there had been no
time to waste on names until now — relaxed back in the
hospital bed as Jennie brought her some tea and
sponged away the stains of blood from her thighs. She
put another fresh paper sheet down. 'But that bleeding
really has almost stopped.'

An hour later, the ambulance arrived and Jennie
accompanied the two patients along some miles of
winding roads back to the Hamilton area, while Mrs
Brady and Mr Heilpern shared a taxi. Her impressions
of Bermuda's King Edward Memorial Hospital were
necessarily brief, as Jessica and the older man were
immediately whisked away by the hospital's own staff,
but the place seemed airy and pleasant, with the lush
grounds of the island's botanical gardens near by.

After half an hour in the foyer coffee shop, she was
joined by a cheerful David Heilpern. 'We saw the baby
on the sonogram and everything is fine. But they've
recommended that Jessica take it easy for the rest of

the cruise. Will you be coming back in the taxi with us?'

'I'd like to, but I want to wait and hear the news about Mr Brady,' Jessica explained, adding, 'I'm so pleased about the baby.'

'We hardly dared to believe it at first, even after Dr Gray's reassurance.'

'Where is she now?'

'Still lying down. They want to play it safe and transfer her by wheelchair to the taxi when it arrives.'

Mrs Brady found them waiting for their transport, her face telling a gloomier story than David Heilpern's had. 'They're admitting him. I'm going to stay. I'll spend the night here at the hospital and move to a hotel in Hamilton tomorrow. They don't want to risk flying him to New York until Monday at the earliest, after some detailed tests here. It's. . .it's probably for the best. He's been resisting the idea of heart trouble for a long time and I've been frightened about what might happen. Perhaps now, with this scare, he'll try and take on a safer lifestyle.'

Jennie could only murmur some sympathetic words. The taxi had arrived and was waiting for them.

Afterwards, this day stood out very clearly in Jennie's mind. In the weeks that followed, she saw many patients, and the way that they came briefly into her life before disappearing forever at the end of their holiday made the details of their faces, names and treatments blur into a tangle. And yet this day stood out clearly, and she found herself wondering quite often about Jessica Heilpern and Chester Brady, hoping that the pregnancy was proceeding smoothly and that the heart condition was undergoing successful treatment. Steven Waxman, too. Was he all right? Had he come to understand the real danger he had been in?

No real difficulty in working out why this should be so, and the reason became more obvious as time went by: it was the day after Anthony's kiss, and the last time they had been at ease with each other. Funny, really. You would have thought that awkwardness would have been at its height that day, and, with time, would have ebbed into an easy friendliness, but actually it was the opposite.

He didn't suggest any more outings together during their free days in Bermuda. In fact, she suspected that he deliberately arranged for her time off to coincide with Hector's rather than his own, and since Hector was almost always in the happy thrall of a new romance by the third or fourth day of the cruise *he* didn't suggest a shared expedition either.

Not that Jennie spent all of her free time alone. There was a loosely knit group of casino, boutique and entertainment workers with whom she got on well, and two or three of them were usually free for an afternoon beach trip or an evening drink in one of the quieter pubs.

Today, though, on her. . .she had to stop and count carefully, then was surprised at the answer. . .eleventh day off in Bermuda—goodness, had she been on the *Leeward* for nearly three months already?—she *was* alone. Perhaps that was why she was mulling unproductively over the issue of Dr Anthony Gray.

She had come to Fort Hamilton today after a morning of shopping, as grey clouds threatened rain and the beach held no appeal. It was her first visit to the old fort, long disused but restored as a tourist attraction that most tourists didn't find time to see, and she found that the place just suited her mood. Suited it too well, perhaps.

The dry moat, cut deeply into the bedrock surrounding the fort, had been made into a lush tropical garden

threaded with an enticing pathway, and she was alone
as she made the five-sided circuit. No, not quite alone.
Several tawny hens and a rooster clucked and scuttled
among the undergrowth, too used to noisy visitors to
be put off by the quiet tread of one solitary young
woman.

Still, a clutch of poultry was not much of a distraction
to thoughts which persistently returned to the subject
of Anthony Gray, try as she might to insist to herself
that there was nothing in their relationship that needed
thinking *about*.

There was nothing in their relationship at all, in fact.
Scenes kept returning to her, tiny ones. Not even
scenes, but moments that repeated themselves with
slight variations week after week. Was it coincidence
that he so often seemed to be sitting down to a meal in
the staff mess just as she arose from one? Or to be
rising just as she was sitting down? And those smoky
grey eyes of his. She never seemed to see them at all.
Just one example. . .

'Jennie, could you get me the file on last year's
juvenile diabetic group? I want to see if any particular
problems cropped up during their cruise, because a
similar group is due on board next week.' A pleasantly
toned request that seemed to be issuing from the top of
his dark head, bent very intently over the notepad on
his desk. . .which was completely blank.

'Not that I'm any different,' Jennie told a curious
rooster as it popped a pert little head out at her from
behind the thick, glossy leaves of some unlikely-looking
tropical shrub. 'I never look at him, never talk to him
if I can help it.'

Why? Too scared! She felt that — slowly — her
emotional state was returning to normal. Ralph Caine
seemed distant, less powerful in her memory. She
hadn't heard from him and didn't want to. She had had

three mild attacks of panic over her responsibility to patients and had overcome them, accepted them, tried not to dwell on them. She just didn't want anything or anyone to rock the boat, to disrupt this careful and delicate healing inside her. . .

And somehow she sensed that if she let Anthony Gray get close to her at all she might find that, instead of this slow draining away of the past and its problems, a whole new set of calamitous feelings might come rushing out all at once. Far too hard to handle. A sudden end to the whole point of running away.

'So I shouldn't blame him for the distance between us. It's necessary. For him, evidently, as much as for me.'

She completed the circuit of the ravine-like moat and climbed some inner stone stairs to explore the time-worn structure of the fort itself. A doorway led to a long gallery — cut into solid rock, it appeared — where armaments and other things must once have been stored. At first it was interesting and pleasant to enjoy the sudden coolness and shade, and to marvel at the work that had gone into the place, but then something in the atmosphere changed.

Idly thinking, This would be a great setting for a Gothic novel or a horror film, Jennie turned a corner into another long, damp gallery. Her eye was caught by a movement at the far end, but when she took a proper look there was nothing. . .and no one. . .there.

A small shiver ran down her spine. Who were the men that had worked and lived here? Had they been happy? Or did past sorrows haunt. . .?

'Nonsense!' she hissed aloud. 'It's just another sight-seer, like me. Keep going.' And she did. Determinedly. Gritting her teeth. Thinking of the *unscariest* things she could. . .like flowers, sunshine, food.

It was no good. Three-quarters of the way down the

next gallery, she stopped, turned and began to go back the way she had come, walking at first, then loping, then frankly and breathlessly sprinting, helter-skelter round the corner, down the second gallery, desperate to see the familiar entrance she had used and utterly certain that those rhythmic sounds she heard were not the echoes of her own flying footsteps but the rapid strides of someone. . .or something. . .in hot pursuit.

Suddenly, a dark shape loomed in the doorway of a side-gallery, a place she had not yet investigated. The ghost? The murderer himself, who had somehow taken a short-cut and. . .?

Before she could stop her headlong terrified rush towards it, she had cannoned hard into the all too solid human figure and was seized by two strong arms.

'Steady on, Jennie.'

'Oh, it's you!'

Weak with shock, Jennie looked up into the face of Anthony Gray, and for a moment she was so relieved that he was actually made of flesh and blood, and not stalking her with nefarious intent, that she fell against his chest and rested her head there, breathing like a steam train. He felt very solid, very steady, and somehow very familiar, with the soft cotton fabric of his shirt like a gentle caress against her skin and the scent of him very masculine yet surprisingly sweet.

'A little bit spooked, were you?' There was a low, rich vibration against her ear as he spoke, and his hands chafed lightly across her back.

'Not at all!' she began indignantly, then, laughing, she lifted her head, stepped backwards out of his too comforting arms and admitted, 'I was completely and utterly terrified, if you want the truth!'

He laughed too. 'A Scottish sixth sense?'

'I hope not! I hope there was no *sense* to it at all! If I thought I really had been *sensing* something that was here. . .' She gave a brief, uncontrollable shiver and saw his slaty grey eyes narrow as he dropped the teasing tone.

'Come up to the top,' he said. 'There's a magnificent view, and with any luck we'll get a break in the clouds and the sun will be shining on the grass.'

'Yes, I'd heard there was a view,' Jennie said briskly. 'This place is interesting, isn't it?'

He wasn't completely fooled by her tone and she was grateful for the reassuring hand lightly placed in the small of her back.

'It *is* interesting,' he said. 'I've been here twice before, but didn't have time to see these passages.'

'More intent on tanning in the sunshine?' she teased.

'It's peaceful up there,' he answered seriously. 'And usually quiet.'

'A good place to play your flute?' It was the first time she had mentioned the subject to him, although by this time she had often heard those ethereal sounds that barely carried through the wall between their two cabins.

He gave her a sidelong look and said, 'I don't disturb you with it, I hope, when I play in my cabin.'

'Not at all.'

'Good. I find it relaxing to play. . . But no, I don't bring the flute up here. It's a good place to think though.'

'Whereas these passages seem to do the thinking for you,' she said with a last shiver. 'Only they don't think my kind of thoughts!'

'What fascinates me is the work that must have gone into these,' he answered. 'This is solid rock.' He touched a musty wall with the open palm of his capable hand. 'I've done some stonemasonry myself and it's damn hard work, hour after hour, even with the help of modern tools and equipment.'

'Stonemasonry? You? As a hobby, or. . .?'

He laughed. 'A hobby? No! As a job. For six months.'

She assumed that this must have been in his late teens on leaving school and said, 'It's funny what ideas kids have about what would make a fun holiday job, isn't it? Still, I expect the reality of the work made the grind of medical studies a lot more palatable a prospect.'

'Hmm.' A growl more than an answer, and she saw that his mood had darkened. He was walking a little ahead of her now and as he reached up to touch the pattern of marks that the tools had made in the stone she saw, under his casual khaki shirt, the muscles rippling in his back. A stonemason for six months! Suddenly, those muscles told their own story and she knew that he wasn't speaking of a long-ago, youthful experience, but of a relatively recent one, perhaps immediately before he had come to work on the *Leeward* just over a year ago.

Shivering again, she followed him up the last flight of stairs and at last they were out into the air and sunshine with the threatening galleries behind them.

'Come over here,' he called to her, racing ahead as if he needed the movement to shake off an unwanted mood. 'You can see the ship, the harbour, the hospital on the hill there across the water. . .'

Clearly, and very typically, he didn't want to be questioned any further about stonemasonry. In fact, he was probably sorry that he had let the information slip in the first place. Respecting a need for privacy that she understood only too well, Jennie followed his lead.

'It *is* a good view,' she said. 'And goodness, I knew the *Leeward* was huge, but I didn't realise that she dominated the skyline so completely. Even all the way up here, I feel I could almost step across to her top deck. She's like a second city, just parked next to Hamilton.'

'Yes, she is impressive. Understandable if locals sometimes resent the swarms of holidaymakers that she disgorges every week, even though their livelihoods depend on tourism.'

They talked and explored some more, and when each discovered that the other had brought sandwiches and fruit juice for a light picnic lunch it seemed natural that they should find a spot and sit to eat together.

But if he's in the habit of coming up here when he wants to think, then I mustn't do the same, Jennie thought during a silence as they ate. It would be too awkward to encounter him again.

Unfairly, she was irritated at Hector for asking for tomorrow off instead of today. It was this request that had brought Dr Gray's schedule into phase with her own, but the Colombian doctor could scarcely be blamed for that. He hadn't done it on purpose. As usual, he had been pursuing his own pleasure, and she very much doubted whether he had given a thought to anyone else's plans.

'People are funny, aren't they?' she said to Anthony, speaking the thought aloud quite naturally as if it followed on from something they had just been talking about, instead of coming from a peaceable silence.

'They are indeed,' he agreed. 'But why this minute, in particular? Are you thinking of me? Or yourself? Or that woman over there, dutifully inspecting a cannon and wearing those rather unfortunate shorts?'

She laughed. 'Not her. Hector, actually, and his conquests. To us he seems like such an open book——'

'And, frankly, not a terribly interesting one, after a while,' he drawled.

She nodded and went on, 'But evidently his lady-friends don't agree.'

'Hector does have a certain talent in performing the role of fascinating Latin lover, but of course he's off-stage when he's with us, so. . .'

'I suppose that's it. In a strange way with us he's very straightforward. I can't help liking that in him, in spite of everything.'

'And yet you're not very straightforward youself, Jennie.'

Their eyes met with telling understanding and she answered him slowly. 'That's not quite true. . .not quite fair, Anthony Gray, and you know it.'

'Straightforward was the wrong word.'

'Then find the right one, please, in case I disagree with that, too.'

'How about forthcoming?'

'All right.' Her cheeks had coloured. 'No, I'm not. Not at the moment. And neither are you. I thought that was what. . .'

She trailed off uncomfortably and he finished for her, 'What we liked in each other? What made us so comfortable together that first day when I took you out?'

'Yes.' Her answer was a low, throaty syllable, and as their eyes met again she knew that their kiss was suddenly as vivid and disturbing a memory to him as it was to her.

'Somehow it never stays comfortable, though, does it?' he went on with inexorable honesty. 'We keep straying into territory that both of us would rather steer clear of. So we seem to have decided to steer clear of each other instead.'

'Is that what's been happening over the last two and a half months?' she answered lightly.

'I think so. Don't you. . .? Have you finished your lunch?'

'Yes.'

'And are you heading back? It's beginning to look like rain again.'

'Yes, it is. I think I *will* go back. I'd thought of doing some more shopping, but that can wait.'

'Then let's go together, and on the way we can practise talking about safer subjects, like women in unfortunate shorts. . .'

'Or spooky underground passages. . .'

'Or Hector Mendez. There must be plenty of such subjects for friends to discuss. . .because I *would* like to be friends with you, Jennie. I don't enjoy avoiding you, as we've both been doing.'

The words were lightly spoken, but something in his eyes compelled a serious response, and she found that her answer came in a low, surprisingly vibrant tone that belied the simplicity of the words. 'Yes, I'd like it, too.'

'Then we're agreed.' Again, it was light, but contained a note of satisfaction. 'My goodness, that's a bizarre and not very welcoming sign on that pub door just there, isn't it?'

'Where?' she asked inanely. His abrupt change of subject had left her somewhat breathless.

'Just here. Hadn't noticed it before.'

They stopped and read the sign together, chuckled briefly at its lengthy and virulent descriptions of the hair and clothing styles that would *not* be tolerated within the establishment and went on their way. The subject of their friendship was closed, it seemed, but all the way back to the ship Jennie had the uncomfortable feeling that Anthony had very firm intentions about what such a friendship would entail and what its limits would be. Unfortunately, she had no idea what those intentions or limits were, and clearly he did not plan to tell her.

CHAPTER SIX

I'D LIKE to see Dr Mendez, please.' The indeterminate American accent was crisp and rather loud three days later in the small waiting-room of the ship's hospital.

In the few seconds that Jennie had to assess the tall, middle-aged man before she replied, she decided that he was either very worried or very angry. But he had asked to see a doctor, so it wasn't up to her to work out which.

'Actually, it's Dr Anthony Gray on duty this evening, not Dr Mendez,' she told the visitor, adding, 'He's our senior doctor,' in case this fact might reassure him.

It didn't. 'Well, I want to see Dr Mendez.' The pitch of his voice rose several decibels and now it was very evident that anger, not anxiety was fuelling him.

'Is it a medical problem?' she queried, perhaps unwisely.

The grey-haired American exploded. 'No, it is not! Neither is it any of your damned business, and if Dr Mendez isn't here, then tell me where I can find the man before this whole medical set-up has a lawsuit on its hands!'

The surgery door opened smoothly at that moment, and Jennie turned to Anthony Gray with frank relief. She didn't need to say anything. He appeared to have heard it all through the closed door. The visitor's words had certainly been loud enough to make it an easy eavesdropping.

'If you have any sort of professional complaint against Dr Mendez, Mr. . .?'

'Herb Nicholson,' growled the angry man.

'Mr Nicholson, then as his superior officer I am also responsible,' Anthony said, sounding very English and very much in command. 'So perhaps we should discuss the matter without him being present?'

Jennie had never heard Anthony refer to himself as Hector's 'superior officer' before, but technically it was true and typically it was just the right touch.

The American grew a little calmer and a little less red-faced. 'Yes, let's just see what action you're going to take.'

'Very well, why don't u come into——?' began Anthony, but he stopped abruptly as two women entered the waiting-room. It was immediately evident that they were the angry man's family, and both involved in the story, whatever it was.

'I found her in the gym, having a massage,' the older woman said to Anthony's antagonist. She pushed the younger woman forward. . .just a girl she was, really, Jennie could now see, in the unforgiving fluorescent lighting. It was a rough, rather disgusted push, and the girl gave a sniffle and a defiant toss of the head.

'A massage?' the girl's father queried in tones of disgust that matched his wife's attitude. 'And how much will *that* add to my credit card tab for the week? Another fifty bucks?'

'Thirty,' the girl muttered, sullen and frightened at the same time. 'It was therapeutic. You know I've been having that trouble with my lower back since——'

If she had hoped to distract her father from the real business of this scene, then she failed dismally.

'Look at the girl! She's sixteen, although I now understand she's been claiming to be just a little older!' He was addressing Dr Gray, evidently forgetting about going into the surgery for privacy.

No one else was waiting, but they were now two hours out of St George's harbour on the return trip to

New York and the seas were unusually rough and grey for midsummer. By now Jennie knew from experience that it was only a matter of minutes until green-faced passengers in dire need of seasickness remedies began making their way down here. Tactfully, she retreated to a position behind the desk in the dispensary and pretended to absorb herself in some paperwork, leaving the door open so that she could be on the alert for new patients and intercept them.

'Sixteen!' the American was repeating with greater outrage. 'And this Hector Mendez of yours has been squiring her round all this week. Casino, nightclub, bars in Hamilton and St George's. If he's interfered with her. . . I want her medically examined to see if —'

'Daddy! Don't be ridiculous!' the girl burst out. Her pretty but rather vacuous blue eyes had widened in horror. 'I don't need to be medically examined. I won't be. If you want the truth, it's very simple. Hector and I are in love. What's wrong with that? Why must you *embarrass* me with this stuff? Just because you found out I didn't get back to my room until three this morning. Serve you right for dumping me in that minuscule cabin on Deck Five with my bratty cousins while you guys loll in luxury on Deck Nine! Hector and I are deeply *in love*, I tell you! No doubt you two have forgotten what the words even *mean*!'

'In love? Oh, my lord!' the father groaned, then he rounded helplessly on Anthony once again, ignoring the restraining hand and murmured words of his wife.

'Herbert, honey. . .'

'What the damn hell are you going to do about it, Gray? I want her medically examined,' he repeated wildly.

In her unwilling position as audience to all this, Jennie bit her lip. Beneath his anger, the man was clearly helpless. She could see now that, brushing aside his talk of lawsuits and medical examinations, he didn't have a clue how to handle the situation, and she only hoped that Anthony did.

Of course he did. 'Please tell me if I understand the situation correctly,' he said calmly and not unsympathetically. 'Dr Mendez and your daughter. . .'

'Melanie,' the mother supplied.

'Melanie and Dr Mendez,' Anthony began again, 'have become involved in a shipboard romance, which——'

'Don't call it that!' Melanie came in passionately. 'We're *in love*, why doesn't anyone *understand* that?'

'Which you, as her parents, are unhappy about because of the age-difference between them, and because of the suddenness with which this has happened. And you are also concerned that, physically, the relationship has gone beyond the level of intimacy that you——'

'Gone beyond the——! Mom, Dad! Please! *Why* did you have to pollute this by——? It hasn't "gone beyond" anything!'

'You've summed it up, Doc,' the father growled. 'Now what are you going to do about it?'

'I'm going to speak to Dr Mendez, of course.' He began to walk confidently to the surgery door, stopping on the way to instruct Jennie, 'Page Hector, would you?'

'Yes, Dr Gray,' she murmured, still feeling that it was best to remain as unobtrusive as possible.

'When he comes,' Anthony addressed the emotional trio once again, 'I'd like, as his superior officer. . .' that useful phrase again, Jennie noted '. . .to speak to him alone. Meanwhile, if you'd all like to step into the privacy of the surgery, we can resolve the question of this medical examination.'

His eyes slid from their fearless command of the Nicholsons' collective gaze to the waiting-room entrance, where the first of the evening's seasick passengers was weaving her queasy way in. The Nicholsons were all much too overwrought to feel seasick. Agitatedly, they followed the doctor and the surgery door was shut behind them.

After quickly lifting the phone to page Hector, Jennie began to take down some details about the unhappy new patient. She was elderly and taking several prescription medicines already, so Jennie noted those as they would influence which seasickness remedy Anthony elected to prescribe. She also gave the usual soothing advice about fresh air and sensible eating.

'I'm afraid you'll have to wait for the doctor, though,' she finished sympathetically. 'He has—um—other patients.'

The silver-haired woman—rather a sweetie, she seemed, a small dumpling in shape and holidaying enthusiastically alone—sat patiently to wait, then the waiting-room door opened again and Hector came in, a groan already framed on his lips.

'That was quick,' Jennie said.

'Oh, I was on my way in already. Darling Jennie, I have the most vile headache and I knew there'd be aspirin here. My lady love and I slipped out to St George's before lunch for a cocktail,' he confided, lowering his voice so that the waiting patient wouldn't hear. 'I shouldn't do that. It's always fatal for my head, but——'

'Your lady love,' Jennie broke in warningly, 'is in the surgery right now—with her parents.'

'Her *parents*?' His face suddenly paled. A comical sight, really, except that Jennie was growing genuinely worried about the situation. Voices of both sexes had been rising and falling behind the surgery door for the past few minutes. At the moment, she couldn't hear anything, but. . . 'Her *parents*!' Hector repeated, sinking into a chair. His Colombian accent had strengthened. 'She told me she was here only with cousins. Cousins of her own age.'

'And how old did she tell you she was Hector?' Jennie queried gently.

'Twenty-five.'

'She's sixteen.'

'Sixteen! Impossible. Oh, good grief! She——'

The surgery door opened and out everyone came. Catching sight of Hector, both parents glared but allowed themselves to be ushered towards the exit. Melanie flung a desperate, beseeching backward glance at the Colombian doctor. 'Hector! Darling! Don't let them tell you——'

But she was swept away before she could finish, her cascade of blonde hair now a frenzied mess after manicured fingernails had run distractedly through it.

'Sixteen!' Hector muttered brokenly.

'There's a patient to see you, Dr Gray,' Jennie said, motioning the elderly woman to come forward.

No reason to make her wait through what might be a long scene between the two doctors. Anthony was soon able to send Mrs Panitski away with the appropriate remedy. Hector, meanwhile, had been whispering feverishly to Jennie, 'Twenty-five, she told me. Of course I believed her! In the nightclub, in the casino, she was heavily made-up, glamorously dressed. She seemed. . .sophisticated. Any childishness I put down simply to freshness, zest for life. Even today in St George's I had no idea. Believe me, Jennie, no idea at all! These ridiculous American parents! A girl of her age should be chaperoned, closely watched and *not* permitted to dress like a TV star. My God, how was I to know? What are such parents thinking of?'

The reassuring smile faded from Anthony's face as soon as Mrs Panitski had safely departed, clutching her little sachet of pills. 'You'll be pleased to hear, Hector,' he began, 'that, with the support of Melanie herself, I was able to persuade Mr and Mrs Nicholson that a medical examination to establish their daughter's virtue was unnecessary.'

If possible, Hector became even paler. 'You mean. . .to establish that I had not slept with her? Thank God I didn't! I was planning. . .tonight. . .the most romantic mutual seduction. I thought she wanted. . .'

'She probably did. . .and does,' Anthony came in drily. 'She told us all more than once that you and she were in love.'

'*Deeply* in love,' Jennie added with emphasis. At this stage she really did feel that Hector Mendez deserved a certain degree of suffering.

'In love?' the Colombian groaned. 'Oh, no! No! I thought she understood. A flirtation. A meeting of souls and then we pass on. She never said. . .'

'But what did *you* say, Hector?' Anthony asked crisply. 'That she was beautiful, no doubt. That this meeting was fated, magic. That you had never felt like this before.'

'But that is true! Each woman is different. That is why——'

Mercilessly, the senior doctor went on, 'Do you really think that to a girl of sixteen——?' He broke off impatiently. Two more seasick passengers were coming in. 'Jennie we're going to shut ourselves away and thrash this out here and now,' he muttered rapidly. 'Do as much as you can for these people and anyone else who comes in, unless it's urgent, of course. Tell people we're having an important case conference about a patient in Intensive Care. There'll be rumours flying all over the ship about it in half an hour, but that can't be helped. Better that the gossip is about a supposed patient than about what's really going on. I still haven't fully defused the lawsuit issue.'

Hector, on overhearing this last part, groaned brokenly once again and muttered, 'Believe me, I am cured of women forever!' as he and the senior doctor disappeared into the surgery.

Jennie put on a bright face and saw to the other patients, placating three more who entered a few minutes later as well. At this rate, the waiting-room would be alarmingly full by the time the two doctors emerged. . .

It was. The men had spent ten minutes alone together and now there were seven green-gilled people waiting. Straining to hear voices from the surgery, Jennie had heard only indistinct tones. Anthony's voice was ominous, drumming and low-pitched, interrupted only occasionally by the higher-pitched and more emotional cadences of Hector's accent. Odd that it should be the Englishman who was doing most of the talking. Normally, with Hector's flowery style, it was the other way around. He had evidently been thoroughly subdued.

Good! Jennie thought.

Dr Mendez remained subdued when the two emerged, and he slunk off with scarcely a word to Jennie. Dr Gray, too, was presenting his most enigmatic professional face, since there was quite a backlog of patients to clear and several new ones arriving.

When finally they were alone, it was almost eight o'clock. Jennie wanted to ask about what was going on, but didn't dare. There was something forbidding about Anthony's expression. . . When the three Nicholsons walked in again just as the surgery was about to close, Jennie understood. Anthony must have been half expecting them.

'Dr Mendez has made a complete explanation and apology, I hope,' he said, coming forward.

'Yes, and my wife has persuaded me to accept it,' Mr Nicholson announced. There was no mistaking the implication. . .that it would not take much for him to throw off his wife's restraint and pursue the lawsuit that he had threatened.

Mrs Nicholson murmured, 'Perhaps in future she won't lie about her age!'

'And he's apologised to you as well, Melanie.' Ignoring the girl's mother — although he probably had some sympathy with her comment — Anthony spoke more gently as he turned to the lovelorn teenager, who looked, if anything, even younger now than the sixteen years her parents claimed for her, and nothing like the twenty-five she had claimed for herself.

There was no reply in words from Melanie. Instead, tears. Her blonde hair was already darkened and dampened into lank rat's-tails, and her eyes were swollen and reddened.

'Sister McDougall, prepare a sedative, would you?' Anthony said, turning to Jennie. In a lower tone, he named a very mild prescription drug. 'Just two doses, orally. It's harmless enough and will give her a good night's sleep.'

Jennie nodded and disappeared into the dispensary, while Anthony wrote out the necessary prescription. She gave a pair of pills to the girl with a plastic cup of water, and gave a sachet containing two more pills to Mrs Nicholson. 'For tomorrow night as well, if she needs it.'

'Thank you, Nurse. I imagine what she really needs is to keep busy,' the mother said sensibly. 'I shouldn't have left her so much to herself this week, but she's so keen to be grown-up. I thought it wouldn't do any harm. It's a pity we're not still in Bermuda, but I'll drag her along to every shipboard activity that's going tomorrow. Craft lessons, bingo, wine-tasting, that napkin-folding contest, you name it. She won't get a chance to mope or sigh. After all, she's only known the wretched man for four days!'

The family departed after Melanie had made a dramatic show of swallowing the sleeping pills.

Anthony shook his head wearily. 'Well, I hope that's the last we'll hear of the thing. I don't like giving out pills as a panacea for the normal emotional traumas of adolescence, but. . .' He didn't finish.

Jennie suggested gently, 'Actually, you don't much like giving out pills for anything, do you?'

'What's that supposed to mean?' he snapped, the sharpness of his anger coming without warning.

Jennie started and stepped back, stammering, 'I—I just meant that you're not one of these doctors who writes out a script for antibiotics at the first sign of a cough or a pimple. I've noticed it and I like it. That's all. Sometimes I feel that the doctors have too much confidence in their medicines and forget all about things like side-effects, long-term consequences, addiction. . .'

'Sorry I snapped.' He had his back to her as he locked the doors of surgery and dispensary, but she could hear that the apology came with difficulty through clenched teeth. Still angry? Or just tense and strained? She had no idea why he should be either and felt ridiculously disappointed and full of regret at having made the comment. She had intended it so innocently, had assumed he would receive it as a mild compliment, had wanted him to know that she was impressed by him as a doctor.

And as a man! On Monday, he had talked about their friendship, and since then she had been enjoying the new feeling of relaxation with him a lot. Now the feeling was gone and part of her wanted to turn on him and shout, If you want us to be friends, then you'll have to learn not to take offence at such a tame remark!

There! Now she was angry as well. Biting her lip and keeping the feeling inside her, she started to leave the hospital, but from behind her he spoke. 'Want to have dinner tonight?'

She stopped and turned, still a little hostile and wary. 'Well, yes,' she said. 'I mean, I'll be heading across to the mess as soon as I've changed, and I expect you will, too. We're a bit late tonight, so. . .'

'I didn't mean in the mess,' he said. 'It's been a difficult evening. I thought you might like to dress up a bit and try second seating with the passengers. I haven't shown myself off in the dining-room in my dress uniform for a while and I'm supposed to. Hell! I'm making it sound as if this is a dreary duty I'm roping you in for.'

'I won't *be* roped in if I don't want to be,' Jennie retorted with spirit, her anger escaping now. 'So don't worry about that! What concerns me is that you might try to bite my head off again the way you did a few minutes ago!'

'Spoil your appetite, would it?' He nodded ruefully. 'I really *am* sorry. I misunderstood your meaning. And the subject of over-prescribing is a sore point. It won't happen again. OK?'

'OK.' She smiled. They were on good terms again. 'Under those conditions, dinner would be lovely.'

'Shall I come next door to your cabin, then, in five minutes and collect you?'

'*Five*?'

'Fifteen,' he amended humbly. 'I did say "dress up", didn't I?'

Jennie did dress up, and it took her longer than fifteen minutes. Unable to resist a shower after the

evening's rather stressful surgery hours, she knew that
he must have been waiting at least ten minutes when
she finally emerged. He looked very elegant standing
there in the corridor, leaning against a wall. The short-
sleeved white shirt of his daytime uniform had been
covered now by an authoritative black jacket, the gold
braid on its epaulettes and sleeves attesting to his status
as a ship's officer. He had shaved, and the lotion he
had applied to the smooth planes of his cheeks and jaw
had a mild, musky flavour that teased but did not
overpower.

Jennie was wearing black, too, a simple but elegant
cocktail frock in a clingy crêpe fabric that felt soft and
sensuous against her clean skin. She had piled her
flame-red hair into a chignon from which fine golden-
glinted tendrils escaped to soften the lines of her neck
and brow, and before either of them had found words
at the sight of each other he reached out and tucked
one wayward strand behind her ear with fingers that
brushed her cheek for a moment as they passed. The
gesture seemed to linger on her skin, as if his fingers
had been coated with some magic, tingling powder.

'Ready?' It was husky, almost a whisper.

'Mmm-hmm,' she nodded, suddenly a little breathless and light-headed. Then, feeling that if they were
friends it was safer to blurt the truth, she found voice
and said, 'Anthony, what is it about a man in uniform?
That jacket is marvellous. I wonder why you don't dine
with the passengers every night just to show it off!'

He laughed. 'I've no wish to acquire liabilities like
Melanie Nicholson, so if you're telling me that the
uniform is Hector's secret weapon I'll never wear mine
again.'

They were late for the eight o'clock seating, but here
the uniform and the authority that came with it were
definitely useful. 'Just a quiet table somewhere, Phil,'

Anthony murmured to the pint-sized but exquisitely proper *maître d'hotel*, also an Englishman.

'I'll put you on the port side,' the *maître d'hotel* replied. 'José only has four people at his table tonight, and a spare table near it, so he'll have plenty of time for you. He's one of our newer waiters but very good.'

José was at their side almost immediately, unfolding the smoky-rose-coloured napkins and laying out menus for them. Most of the other diners had already begun their main courses, and the golden lights of the dining-room had overtaken the purple-toned power of the setting sun now.

Looking around her, Jennie was glad she had dressed with a degree of formality. She saw men in evening suits and women in jewels and long gowns, as well as others as glamorous but less formal in sequinned or beaded mini-length cocktail dresses and dramatically draped silk creations. Waiters came and went on skimming feet, their voices almost reverent as they described the delectable choices on tonight's menu.

As Phil had promised, Anthony and Jennie were seated in a quiet corner, but Anthony's professional responsibilities still intruded. Two of the patients he had seen during the week waved from nearby tables and beckoned him over for a brief chat, and a third, whom Anthony had treated for an indeterminate stomach upset one night when Jennie wasn't on call, sent his card across in José's hands.

'Charles M. King,' Anthony read aloud to Jennie. 'Producer. Of what, I wonder? When someone comes in at one in the morning with abdominal pain and vomiting I don't tend to find out a lot about his personal life.'

'What else is on the card?' Jennie wanted to know, glimpsing several more groups of discreet, impeccable lettering.

'Addresses,' Anthony said, showing her the card. 'Park Avenue in New York. Beverly Hills in Los Angeles, and somewhere in Connecticut that sounds like a rather large estate. '"Rowan Acres."'

'New York and Los Angeles. So this is what they mean by "bi-coastal"?'

'Yes. Evidently he's quite an important man. And look. . .he's coming over.'

Approaching them with the confident stride and bearing of someone who was used to being in command was a solidly built and imposing man who looked about forty-five. He thrust out a hand to Anthony and said, 'Great to see you again, Dr Gray, and in more pleasant circumstances than Sunday night, hey?'

'*Much* more pleasant,' Anthony agreed.

'Although you do have an excellent set-up down there. I was very impressed the other night, let me tell you. Very impressed with you personally as well, I might add.'

José appeared at that moment, carrying their expected appetisers of duck terrine and salmon-spinach roulade, but also an unexpected bottle of something that even Jennie recognised as *very* expensive French champagne.

'I took a liberty,' said Charles King. 'Please. . .' He gestured at José and the bottle was opened before Anthony and Jennie could protest.

Politeness now demanded that they accept and enjoy the glamorous drink, which indeed was light, heady and delicious. Jennie noticed, though, that the producer had not ordered a glass for himself, and Anthony commented on the fact.

'Not for me today.' Mr King shook his head impatiently and slumped a little in the chair he had pulled over to their table. 'To tell the truth, Doctor, I still haven't been feeling too good since Sunday night.'

'You haven't been back to see me,' Anthony pointed out, gently accusing.

'Nothing definite, you see. I wouldn't have known what to tell you. I thought it must be because I'd been less careful about my diet than usual. I had an ulcer five years ago and since then I've been watching how I ate, but of course on a cruise. . . Which is why no champagne tonight. We'll see if that improves things. No reason for you two not to enjoy it, though.'

'Do see your own doctor as soon as you get home,' Anthony replied seriously. 'Especially if this nausea persists.'

'You mean it could be my ulcer coming back?'

'That, or something more serious. I don't want to alarm you. . .but I don't want you to let it slip, either. I know you're a busy man.'

'You can say that again! I was on the phone to Los Angeles for two hours this afternoon. My wife was ready to kill me.' He gestured across the dining-room to where a blonde woman of about half his age was talking with animation to some very glamorous companions. 'But this new film deal is giving everyone the usual headaches. Two stars commit verbally. They love the screenplay. They love the role, et cetera, et cetera. Then they drop out three hours before signing their contracts!'

He shook his head, seized a glass and poured a generous spill of the champagne into it after all, waving away José's offer of help. Probably a good thing that he was taking a share. Anthony and Jennie, being on call tonight, wouldn't have managed to finish half of it alone.

Jennie listened to Charles King's complaints and effusions about the film and television industries for some minutes more as she finished her terrine, soup and salad, encouraged through each delicious course by

Mr King's extravagantly waving hands. 'Go on! Eat up! Don't bother about me!'

It was a fascinating glimpse into a very unreal world, and when he finaly left as their main courses arrived she had reached the realisation that he must be a very wealthy and important man in his own sphere.

'Did you enjoy that?' Anthony asked a little tentatively as they cut into tender steak.

'Yes, I did, actually,' she assured him. 'The world of Hollywood isn't one I'd like to inhabit permanently, but small glimpses into it every now and then are rather exciting.'

'True,' Anthony laughed. 'And Charles M. King seems genuine enough in his own way. He didn't seem to expect any special treatment the other night in the surgery, in spite of his VIP status.'

'You sound as if you would have been quite prepared to give it to him,' Jennie commented carefully. The senior doctor's words had sent a small chill over her, with their reminder of Ralph Caine telling her how Sir Peter Farrow was a very important man who merited special attention. That painful echo of memory again. . .

And what was Anthony saying? 'I'd have had to give him special treatment if he'd made a fuss. My instructions from the company are very clear on that point. The luxury service that passengers expect on the *Leeward* must be extended to their treatment in our hospital.'

'But you, personally,' Jennie probed. Somehow, the answer that Anthony Gray would give to this question seemed very important. 'Do you think that someone should receive better medical care in a hospital — a big hospital, say — because they are paying more? Better *medical* care,' she stressed. 'I'm not talking about more elaborate meals and prettier curtains at their windows.'

'Of course I don't,' he exploded when she had finished, seeming indignant that she could even suggest such a thing. 'What? You're saying I can get away with washing my hands less thoroughly before examining an indigent patient with AIDS, whereas Mr John P. Important gets three specialists in sterile gowns and caps to be checked for an ingrown toenail?'

'No, *I'm* not saying it,' she came in. 'But there are people who would.'

'Money and power. Is that all medicine boils down to these days?' he muttered angrily, before jabbing his steak with an aggressive fork.

The exchange, blowing up unexpectedly out of idle conversation about Charles King, put a storm cloud over their meal for a while, but it gradually cleared and Anthony said gently, 'No more talk about medicine, all right? I didn't mean to jump on you like that, but what made you think——?' He stopped. 'Never mind. I've worked with indigent patients. Unattractive and unpleasant people, some of them, as you meet in all walks of life, but we all worked harder at that clinic than I'd ever worked before and the care we gave——'

Again he stopped—very abruptly, this time—and frowned. That full, sensuous upper lip of his made his face look very serious, and very sensitive. 'Sometimes, there was a temptation to try and be *superhuman*, to give more hours and more energy than one body could possibly stand. Ultimately, that's *not* good care any more, is it? When a doctor's failings and weaknesses begin to affect his work. . . Perhaps I was kidding myself for longer than I thought.'

Watching him intently, listening, nodding, Jennie became aware that he was speaking less and less to her and more and more to himself, and that his musings, so jerkily and hesitantly worded, were painful ones. It was a chance, she knew, to draw forth revelations from him that she had been curious about since the day they met, but she also knew that she could not do it now, not when he suddenly seemed so vulnerable, more vulnerable than she herself had felt just minutes ago when thinking of Sir Peter Farrow and Ralph. . .

She said quietly, 'Anthony, you promised we weren't going to talk about medicine.'

With an effort he looked up at her and focused his gaze, seeming to draw comfort from the sight of her red-gold hair catching the light on her head and around her face. 'I did, didn't I? Thank you, Genevieve McDougall.'

And for the rest of the meal they talked only of trivial things.

CHAPTER SEVEN

THAT night, they were both on call. Jennie had fallen asleep at midnight after lying awake in her bed for almost an hour.

I shouldn't have let Anthony talk me into that coffee and dessert, she thought more than once as she tangled the sheets and blanket with her restless turning.

But she knew that he hadn't had to talk very hard. It had been a wonderful meal, even after their less than relaxed exchange about medicine and money.

So when, at just after one, the telephone burred insistently from the small chest of drawers that separated her bed from Tilly's and it was Anthony summoning her for work, Jennie stumbled into the bathroom to dress, feeling that she hadn't been to sleep at all.

'Mumps. A crew member,' he summarised quickly when she arrived, his voice lowered. The patient sat slumped on the examining table. Of Middle Eastern origin, he looked pale and ill. 'He's had symptoms since yesterday, but he's fairly new to the ship and he was afraid to say he was sick in case he lost his job. Tonight, though, his cabin-mates saw how thoroughly ill he looked at the end of his evening shift and made him call in.'

'What *is* his job?' Jennie asked. Mumps could be a serious disease in adults, and if the infection spread wholesale among crew, let alone passengers. . .

'He's a cleaner, fortunately. That should do less damage than if he'd been a kitchen hand.'

'And presumably he has his hands in water and disinfectant several times a day.'

'Yes, we've been lucky. But of course he eats in the mess, rooms with other crew members and spends time with friends. . .'

'Quarantine him?'

'We'll have to.' He grimaced.

'Locking the stable door after the horse has bolted?'

'I hope not. Most adults have had it years ago, and most children are immunised these days. Prepare Ward One for him, would you? I've prescribed a couple of things, too. He's feverish and in quite a bit of pain and discomfort. Those parotid glands are hard as rocks.'

'You want me to stay overnight?'

'Yes, please. Take Ward Two to sleep in yourself and dose him again in four hours.'

'You look tired,' she observed as he prepared to leave.

'Yes, I hadn't been able to get to sleep. It was almost a relief when I was paged. I'll take over from you at about six, so you can get back to your cabin for a sleep-in.'

Fifteen minutes later, Jennie was alone in the hospital with the sick crew member, who had stumbled gratefully into the freshly made hospital bed and was already in a half-stupor of illness and sleep. He had taken the prescribed pills hungrily, and would hopefully pass a peaceful night. Jennie wanted to do the same, but again sleep eluded her. Perhaps it was the rather narrow, unfamiliar bed. Perhaps it was her awareness of the ill man in the small room next door. . .

Somehow, though, Anthony Gray was the person who kept filling her thoughts. He had been dressed in his uniform, its shirt slightly crumpled as if he had retrieved it hurriedly from a laundry bag, and his face had worn the creased, papery look of someone who was fighting fatigue. As for his hair. . .even now as she lay here listening to the hum of the engines below, her fingers itched to smooth it back against his well-shaped head. Hours ago in the restaurant, he had looked so perfectly groomed and tailored. Funny. . . Somehow she liked the untidy look even better.

Next door, the patient groaned in his sleep and rolled over, an elbow banging against the wall, then, cutting across the sound, came that of the telephone in the surgery and Jennie hurried to answer it, smoothing the skirt of her uniform as she went. Sleeping in one's clothes never felt right.

'We've been paged again,' came Anthony's voice. 'Charles King. He's on his way down and he'll probably get there before I do, so —'

'I'll be ready for him,' Jennie cut in.

'Good. See you in a few minutes.'

He wasted no more time in talk and Jennie could only assume that the film producer's upset stomach had grown worse. When he arrived just a minute later, this proved to be the case. He was pale, sweaty and doubled over in pain.

'It's all on my left side this time,' he gasped. 'Doesn't feel like the ulcer. Oh, my God, I know it's bowel cancer. My mother died of it.'

Far less suave now than he had been in the restaurant hours before, he looked older than Jennie had thought him then. His young wife was with him, and although she held his hand at intervals and made soothing sounds Jennie could see that the blonde woman was hiding distaste for this whole scene.

I've seen her before, the nurse realised as she made the patient as comfortable as possible in the surgery. Then she remembered a successful American television comedy series she had watched several times in England last year. Mrs King, under her own name, was an actress.

'It's cancer,' Charles King gasped again.

'Of course it isn't, darling,' his wife soothed in honeyed accents, then caught Jennie's glance and rolled her eyes as if this man were an irritating elderly uncle instead of her husband.

Anthony arrived at that moment. Now he had abandoned the slightly crumpled shirt to its fate in the laundry and wore a fresh one, as if he already knew that this would be no brief interruption to his sleep.

'No lessening of the pain, Mr King?' he asked solicitously at once.

'No, it's getting worse. It *must* be cancer, mustn't it?'

'Nonsense,' the Englishman answered briskly. 'From what you've told me over the phone, I'm guessing it's appendicitis, and a classic presentation, too. An examination will tell me more, and then. . .'

'I'll wait outside,' Mrs King came in quickly. Jennie had remembered now that her professional name was Helen Banfield.

'Sweetheart. . .?' her husband groaned.

'I'll only be in the way.' She had slipped out a moment later, looking impossibly fresh and well-groomed for this hour of the night — or rather morning — although she was dressed, like her husband, in a heavy silk dressing-gown.

Anthony washed his hands, Jennie pulled some gloves from a dispenser and handed them to him, and the examination was soon completed.

'As I thought,' the doctor said. Charles King had winced and groaned with each careful palpation.

'Will it go away on its own?' he asked hopefully. 'Some drugs for the pain, and — '

'I'm afraid not. Mr King, we're going to have to operate straight away. That annoying little squiggle at the end of your colon is in danger of perforating before morning as far as I can judge.'

'Operate? Here? Now? Helen. . .! No way, Mr! I

want to be flown off this ship to Cornell Medical Center in New York City immediately or sooner! I want the finest surgeons and the finest care. The tin-pot facilities you have here? And what kind of a doctor are you, anyway, working a cruise ship like some has-been lounge singer?'

Fear had turned the man grey, and anger had tensed every limb. Glancing at his chart, Jennie saw that he was actually ten years older than she had pegged him in the restaurant tonight, and now he looked every bit of those fifty-five years and more. The gracious gesture of champagne and the praise for Dr Gray's talents seemed like a dream now. When it came to the crunch, Charles M. King, Producer, wanted only VIP treatment.

Anthony had flinched visibly at the man's last accusation but his reply was steady and calming. 'We don't have the facilities for air transfer of patients, Mr King, but I assure you that we have everything we need here, including full anaesthesia. Don't forget that this operation has been around since the days of ether and fifty-bed open wards.'

'Don't *patronise* me, Dr Gray,' the man snapped, sitting up then bending over in pain once again.

'That wasn't my intention, I'm sorry.'

'What if I wait till we dock in New York and go by ambulance to —— ?'

'Peritonitis two days from now will be a lot harder to treat even at Cornell Medical Center than surgery will be to do right here and now.'

'Oh, God. . .' he groaned. 'Where did you train? Why on earth *are* you here? Alcohol problem? Failed exams in your speciality?'

'Page Hector,' Anthony told Jennie in a strained aside.

'And Tilly?'

'And Tilly,' he agreed wearily, before turning back to the still suspicious patient.

Jennie went discreetly to the phone to summon the rest of the *Leeward's* complement of medical staff, as Anthony said stiffly, 'Mr King, please be assured that the company who owns this cruise line employs only competent and fully trained doctors and nurses, and runs a thorough background check on their credentials. We have the equipment, the facilities and the staff. . . and peritonitis is a very serious matter. Surely that's all you need to know!'

The producer gave a throaty growl then called, 'Helen!' once again.

His young wife returned reluctantly to the surgery, still holding a fashion magazine from the waiting-room open with her thumb. 'Darling. . .?'

'They're going to operate at once.' It was a melodramatic announcement, but if he had been hoping for a strong reaction he was disappointed.

The actress wrinkled her brow delicately. 'Are they? Poor darling! I had *my* appendix out when I was ten. That's why I've got that horrible scar. I remember I felt real, real yucky for days before and days afterwards. Poor angel! My plastic surgeon says I should have the scar taken care of. What do you think?'

'Go to bed, Helen,' her husband replied heavily. 'Get your beauty sleep. Come and see me in the morning when I look human again.'

The actress — who, given the talk of a plastic surgeon, was perhaps not quite as young as she looked — was clearly relieved at the dismissal, though she said halfheartedly, 'Should I really go? I want to be here *with* you, just *be* with you. . .' Then quickly, 'But all right. If you're sure. I *am* exhausted. I'll see you after breakfast. . .though I doubt you'll be looking *very* human by then.'

She kissed him briefly on the forehead, then drifted thankfully away, taking the magazine from the waiting-room with her. Jennie was thoroughly disgusted with both of them by this time, but there was too much to do to feel anger or weariness or anything else. Equipment and patient to prepare, signed consent form to obtain from him, operating-room to check, sterile gown, cap and mask to put on and a doctor's scrub to assist with as well as her own.

Post-operative care had been Jennie's speciality in England. She hadn't been in Theatre assisting with abdominal surgery for a long time, but somehow everything fell into place and the team was soon ready. Anthony would operate, Jennie would assist, Hector would manage anaesthesia and Tilly would circulate.

It was three in the morning by this time and the rest of the ship was quiet. Even in the casino and nightclub, the last places to close down each evening, passenger ranks would be thinning. Few people, as they danced, gambled or slept, could be aware of the medical drama being enacted down on Deck Three. Even Helen Banfield, if she had finished reading that magazine, was probably asleep.

Charles King was asleep now, too, in the deeper unconsciousness of anaesthesia. Hector was careful with the anaesthesia, adjusting the dose for weight and body type, then Anthony began the procedure, making the normal McBurney skin incision, then dissecting down until he reached the lining of the abdominal cavity.

'Looking good,' Hector commented with slightly forced cheerfulness. He had been embarrassed on greeting everyone tonight, and Jennie realised that he must still be preoccupied with the unfortunate episode of Melanie Nicholson's teenage infatuation. Difficult to

believe that those scenes with the Nicholson family
were still less than twelve hours ago. . .

Next, Anthony lifted out a portion of bowel and
placed it carefully on the sterile drapes that covered Mr
King's abdomen. Jennie laid moist towels over the
delicate tissue, which must not be allowed to dry out.
He examined the intestine carefully.

'No signs of any other disease,' he murmured. Following the small bowel down to where it joined the
large bowel, he soon announced, 'This is it, and I was
right. . .thank goodness.'

'Mr King wouldn't have thanked you for finding a
healthy appendix in there after all this,' Jennie
commented.

'Certainly not!'

They all knew that surgical exploration was the only
way to completely confirm a diagnosis of appendicitis.
False symptoms could occur, but if a doctor was reasonably sure of his suspicions he had to operate. With the
risk of gangrene and peritonitis, better safe than sorry.

In this case, the symptoms had not been false. The
worm-like organ, which had no known function in the
body, was swollen and infected. 'Right where it should
be, too,' said Hector. That was another irritating fea-
ture of the appendix. It would migrate to some unlikely
spot in the abdomen and be quite hard to find. Tonight,
though, no such problems. 'And no Meckel's diverticu-
lum,' Anthony added, referring to secondary kinks in
the bowel which could also become infected.

He freed the organ of any adhesions, leaving it
attached only at the colon, then used sutures to tie
blood vessels that fed it and cut them away. Finally, the
appendix itself was removed by making two sutures
near its base and cutting between them. A suture left
on the colon prevented it from leaking its contents into
the abdominal cavity.

Jennie removed the moist towels and the length of
delicate intestinal tissue was replaced in the abdominal
cavity. A careful count was made to ensure that no
swabs or other items had been left in the wound and
then Anthony carefully and neatly closed it. Jennie
remembered that he had worked in neonatal surgery
for four years. It showed in the meticulous deftness of
his touch.

As Hector began to bring the patient out of anaesthesia, there was a collective lightening of spirits. A
routine operation, but the patient's reluctance and
anger had added a level of tension that none of them
had needed.

A routine operation. . . Thinking the words, Jennie
was struck by their ominous familiarity. She looked
down at the patient, still inert on the table, almost as
immobile and lifeless as death itself. Overlaying this
waxy image was the one of Mr King at dinnertime as
he gestured to their waiter to open the champagne.
Then, he had been relaxed, confident, very sure of his
status, very open about his evident wealth as betrayed
by the casual gift of expensive champagne.

A wealthy, important man undergoing a routine
operation. . .and just yards away in a fevered and
uncomfortable sleep a young man named Ali, a lowly
and unimportant cleaner whom nobody cared about,
except, perhaps, a family hundreds of miles across the
ocean. . .

Leaving the operating-room, Tilly and Hector peeled
off their surgical garb.

'Yes, you two, get back to bed,' Anthony ordered.
'We'll manage the rest.'

It was almost four, and Jennie had barely slept. She
felt tired and tense, and found that she was gritting her
teeth hard. Charles King and Ali the cleaner. Sir Peter

Farrow and Freddy Blount, the indigent, dying old man.

Don't think about it! Don't! There's no similarity. It doesn't matter. No one is going to die. Don't *think* about it! she ordered herself inwardly.

But it was no use. A panic that she had thought was almost conquered rose in her more strongly than ever. Anthony would soon leave her here alone to watch over Mr King's recovery, to check his vital signs and returning bowel sounds. And there was Ali. He was groaning in his sleep again, and soon it would be time to check on his condition and give him more medication. What if, while she was in Ward One with Ali, the far more *important* patient in Ward Two had some crisis and. . .?

'Well, he's settled in for the night,' Anthony said cheerfully. 'Opened his eyes a moment ago, but he's very groggy. I'll take out the IV line when I take over from you at six. Two hours away. And the catheter can stay in until mid-morning.'

He left the tiny ward and headed for the door. Jennie couldn't speak, just nodded at his words as she watched him go. The door shut behind him and the faint hum of air-conditioning started up, overlying the deeper, more subtle note of the ship's huge engines. The two sounds, which she had been unaware of all during the surgery, told her more clearly than anything else that she was alone, and her panic rose to the surface at last, beyond all control.

'Anthony! Anthony!' She wrenched open the door and flung herself after him, catching him up just beyond the bank of lifts.

'My God, what's wrong?'

But Jennie couldn't answer. Sobbing and trembling, she let him take her into the only place where she wanted to be — the shelter of his arms.

'Patients,' he said. 'We can't leave them.'

'I know!' she broke out as he led her back to the hospital. 'We're responsible for them. *I'm* responsible. And what if he dies? What if he *dies*?'

They reached the safety and privacy of the waiting-room and Anthony pulled her down on to the small couch beside him. 'No one's going to die, Jennie.'

'But they do. People do. After routine surgery, sometimes, and when it happens. . .when the nurse who is responsible. . .when the patient is a man who everyone thinks is so important, so —' She broke off, unable to finish the incoherent outpouring.

Without speaking, just murmuring the soothing sounds he might have used to a child, Anthony took her more firmly in his arms and rocked her, letting his body give the reassurance that was so much more powerful than words. At first, Jennie could not give herself to it, her limbs were so stiffened with fear, but gradually he coaxed them to soften and then she was resting against him, drinking in his warmth and his scent.

'Jennie. . . Genevieve. . .' He kissed her forehead with light, soft touches of his lips, then moved down to kiss closed lids, tear-stained cheeks and trembling jaw. She let him, feeling the gentle pressure of each touch like a blessing, and making no attempt either to respond or to pull away.

In the beginning, she didn't even know if it was a gesture of sensuality or simply of comfort and she didn't care, but then, as her panic and distress began to ebb, she felt a stirring of more womanly needs and let a sigh of surrender escape from softly parted lips. He seemed to take it as a sign. . .as indeed it was. . .and a moment later his mouth had covered hers, tasting her and plucking a full, complete kiss from her, like plucking a ripe fruit from a tree.

'Jennie. . .' he said again, a sigh this time, and his palms reached up to cup and caress the oval lines of her face.

When he pulled away, kissing her eyes and cheeks once more, it was such a fluid movement that it didn't feel like a withdrawal at all and his arms came down again to hold her firmly around her slim shoulders.

'What was that about, love?' he whispered.

'Nothing. It's gone now. I've. . .come to my senses,' she answered.

'I think you have to talk about it to me,' he insisted throatily. 'This isn't the first time you've panicked on the job here. It's the worst, but not the first.'

So he had noticed those other times, when she had thought she had so successfully quelled the feelings before anyone else was aware of them! For a moment longer she was silent, almost sullenly so. Let me get over this in my own way, she wanted to tell him. I came away so I wouldn't have to explain, know that people were watching and asking each other questions. 'Is she going to crack? *Was* it her fault? Ralph Caine certainly thought so. . .'

'Jennie, it's why you're here, isn't it?'

And she knew that she had to talk about it to this man.

'Yes. . .'

The story came out. Ralph. . .her pride at the fact that of all the other nurses at the hospital, of all the women he knew, he had chosen *her*. . .his ambition. . . Sir Peter Farrow. . .the dying old man. . .the scenes of anger and betrayal. . . And in telling it aloud she understood it all so much better.

'It made me doubt *everything*. . .and myself most of all. Being with Ralph had distanced me from the other nurses, and I *wanted* it to. Part of me *wanted* to be the wife of an important specialist. So when it all happened

I couldn't talk about it to the other nurses, couldn't get their perspective or their support. They probably all thought that it served me right.'

'Did they really?' he teased gently.

'I don't know! I'll never know. After it happened, I was so lost. . . Ralph didn't really love me, I didn't really love Ralph. I blamed him for the calculating nature of his ambition, and now I see that in my own way I was just as bad. I didn't understand, really, how and why everything could suddenly be so different. It seemed that Sir Peter's death *must* be my fault, since it had changed so much in my life. . . And yet one thing I knew for certain was that it wasn't wrong of me to spend that time with Mr Blount.'

She stopped, needing his agreement in spite of the fervency of what she had just said.

'No, it wasn't wrong.'

'And was it wrong to come away? To drop everything, let my parents think it was just some frivolous wanderlust?'

'Wasn't it you who said it to me that first night when we went out? Sometimes you *have* to run away.'

'Yes,' she agreed ruefully. 'As fast and as far as possible so that what you're running away from doesn't come pelting after you, breathing down your neck.'

'Like your ghost the other day at Fort Hamilton?'

'There is a certain similarity, isn't there?'

'Only this time you've managed to stop running and turn to face it.'

'Have I? I seem to remember that both times the only thing that stopped me was cannoning into *you*!'

'Hmm. Upon which *I* turned you round to face it,' he acknowledged. 'Well, perhaps we all need help sometimes.'

'Do you?' she asked lightly, thinking of the open

secret between them that he was running away from something as well.

'Not now.' Two simple words that closed, for the moment at least, the door of intimacy that had opened once again between them. Not just the intimacy of confession, but that of touch and closeness and sensuality as well.

He was right, though, she acknowledged inwardly. Now was not the time. She pulled away from his arms that still encircled her shoulders and felt horribly bereft of his touch. The salt of her tears — which those kisses of his on her cheeks had not fully wiped away — was dried now, making her skin feel even stiffer than fatigue could make it.

'Go to bed,' she told him, 'and don't come in at six. I'll ring your cabin if there are any problems.'

'Don't be silly,' he answered. 'You're the one who is going to bed. Charles King is *not* going to die, but after what you've told me tonight you don't need the pressure of being alone with him now.'

'Actually, isn't there some idea that you should get straight back on to a horse after you've been thrown?' she managed.

'Not at four-thirty in the morning. I think you've released something tonight, something that was pent up inside you and getting in the way of all sorts of things. Now. . .just sleep it off.'

He almost pushed her out of the door and Jennie couldn't protest any further. She felt drained, as limp as wet paper, and, although she doubted that sleep would come easily, the haven of her cabin and bed beckoned.

He's very generous. . .too generous, she thought as she left Anthony alone. And perceptive, patient. . .

And I'm falling in love with him.

Perhaps it shouldn't have come as such a shock.

After all, he had kissed her twice and each time the sensations that his mouth and caressing hands had aroused within her were so rich and so delightful. . . But it wasn't the kisses, the dark mystery of his looks, the masculine strength and scent of him. It's just *him*, she realised. And I *can't* let it happen! I know nothing about him!

Whereas she had known everything about Ralph Caine. That was, everything that was superficial and nothing that was truly important. She had known Ralph's background, the course of his education, his future plans, his parents and his family home. She knew none of this about Anthony Gray, just scattered, enigmatic clues like a paper chase spoiled by the wind.

He had been a stonemason, he had worked in neonatal surgery under Stephen Greer, now he was an unimportant GP on a holiday cruise liner, his mother wrote to him on pale pink paper and signed herself 'Mummy', he got migraine headaches which he hated and was trying to cure. . .and he was running away.

He could have been anything, done anything in England, she told herself harshly. Been a psychiatric patient, sabotaged someone else's career, beaten his girlfriend, cooked the hospital books and left before he was caught. . . All sorts of possibilities that might never have shown up in the shipping company's background check.

And it didn't matter. There was something about him. . .different from anything she had ever felt for Ralph. In one moment of blinding confidence, she knew that she trusted him absolutely. And in the next moment she realised that trust was not the issue.

He's not looking for love out here. I wasn't either. . .but now that it's starting to happen I *want* it. He doesn't. It took him nearly three months even to be willing to be friends!

'Not now.' The words he had spoken to her a few minutes ago took on an added meaning. No kisses, no passionate discovery, no love in his life. Not here on the *Leeward*. Not now.

But that could change, couldn't it? her heart insisted.

Opening the door of her cabin quietly, Jennie scolded herself wearily. Go to bed and get some sleep, girl. Perhaps all of this will seem ridiculous in the morning.

CHAPTER EIGHT

'RIDICULOUS'. 'Ridiculous' would have been nice, followed by 'unimportant' and finally 'forgotten'. It didn't happen, but so much else *did* that Jennie had little time to think or feel or mull.

Charles King passed a comfortable night and began to recover as expected, rather subdued, showing his age, and casting no more aspersions on the quality of their facilities and care. Helen Banfield made frequent brief, fluttery visits to her husband, ordering all sorts of special attentions for him. . .but she never returned the magazine. It was rather a relief on Saturday morning when an ambulance came to spirit the post-operative patient away to Cornell Medical Center.

The film producer was soon forgotten, however. Over the next four weeks, mumps moved steadily and inexorably through the ranks of the crew, despite all the efforts that Dr Gray took in directing the hygiene precautions on board. All crew members were given a skin test to ascertain whether they were susceptible to the disease or already immune. Those who were not immune were given a mumps immune globulin, but for many it was already too late. The disease took two to three weeks to develop, and they had already been exposed.

Also, everyone was interviewed and asked whether they had had the disease as children, but this information was sometimes difficult to obtain, as some crew members' English didn't extend to such words as 'mumps', let alone 'swelling of the parotid glands'.

Some of the less educated crew members were reluc-

tant about immunisation until it was explained to the
men that in rare cases—the rarity was stressed—the
disease could spread to the testicles and cause sterility.
Other crew members had heard of this complication
and their panic had to be carefully allayed.

Somehow—and Jennie believed it was purely
through the rigorous hygiene precautions that Anthony
oversaw—they managed to keep the illness confined to
crew members, and few passengers even knew that
there was a problem. The five tiny wards down in the
ship's hospital were full, or nearly so, for much of the
time, however. Eight patients one week, seven the
next, then nine, and four the week after that. It was an
exhausting time, with a doctor or nurse rostered on
duty twenty-four hours a day in addition to their normal
unpredictable workload.

When Jennie wasn't working, she ate or slept, and
when she *was* working it was often difficult to keep the
patients happy and provide for all their needs,
especially when language was a problem.

When the fifth week of the outbreak came and their
complement of patients was down to two, Anthony
pronounced the crisis past and there was a collective
sigh of relief. 'Take some time off this afternoon when
we're in New York,' Anthony told Jennie during an
early morning meeting to discuss the situation. 'If you
can get off the boat by ten, I won't need you again until
after two. That's four hours. You too, Hector.'

'No, no,' the Colombian doctor insisted, with a wave
of his hand. 'You take the time, Anthony. I am happy
to be rostered on.'

'But you haven't set foot on shore in two weeks!'

'Unimportant. Unimportant,' Hector insisted, with
his usual extravagance and breezy tone. 'Perhaps I will
find time this week in Bermuda.'

Since the episode of Melanie Nicholson—about

whom, fortunately, no more had been heard since she left the ship at the end of her cruise — he had been very anxious to display his dedication to the job.

'A well-timed burst of enthusiasm,' Anthony had drawled rather cynically to Jennie one day, 'in view of our load lately.'

But in spite of everything Jennie was inclined to be more forgiving towards Hector. 'He *is* doing the work, though,' she had pointed out to Anthony. 'It's not just for show. He has a terrific rapport with the crew members, he's put in more hours than any of us, and I don't think he's looked at a blonde in four weeks.'

'Hmm. Probably planning a switch to redheads. . .'

'Are you sure, Hector?' Anthony said now.

'Very sure. New York at this time of year! Hot, dirty, no time to do anything but buy toothpaste and aerogrammes.'

'True.' The senior doctor laughed. 'And those are just the things I need, so thank you, I *will* take the time myself.'

Accordingly at ten that morning, Jennie was not surprised when she met up with Anthony in the short queue that had formed at the crew's disembarkation checkout. He was dressed casually in light khaki jeans and a white shirt, while Jennie wore a lemon-yellow sundress, as Hector was right about the weather in New York today: it was mid-August, and it was *hot*!

'Are you on the toothpaste trail, too?' he teased.

'No. I stocked up several weeks ago on all those things. You're right though, they're far cheaper here than on board ship or in Bermuda. I'm more interested in yoghurt and muesli today. The passengers only have to eat that delicious rich food for a week. A constant diet of it is telling on my taste-buds and my digestion!'

'Shall we track it all down together?'

'Why not?'

She tried not to show how absurdly pleased she was at his suggestion. Tried *especially* not to show the sudden, nervous fluttering feeling inside her. But, It's hopeless! she admitted to herself. I *am* falling for him. If four weeks of mumps couldn't cure me, what can?

Knowing that she should be running a mile from these feelings, and running a mile from *him*, she couldn't help feeling a delicious sense of freedom and happiness at the idea of venturing off into this great city with the man. Part of her wanted to fight against this, deny it, spoil the day for herself and probably for him by being distant and careful. The rest of her. . .most of her. . .didn't care.

'No sense in burdening ourselves with grocery bags straight away,' Anthony said as they walked up towards the centre of Manhattan from the rather dingy West Side streets, made famous by Leonard Bernstein's musical. 'Let's target a promising-looking supermarket and drugstore and come back to them later, at about a quarter-past one.'

'And till then?'

'Explore. And have lunch.'

'I like it.'

Even the heat couldn't spoil the morning. They went as far as Fifth Avenue, window-shopped at Tiffany's, went into Trump Tower and travelled up four flights of escalators amid a welter of marble and gold. . .and an indoor waterfall. They didn't buy anything. Little girls' velvet dresses for seven hundred dollars or outrageous women's hats for three hundred and fifty dollars didn't seem like an urgent priority today.

Next they tried FAO Schwartz's famous toy store, where stuffed zoo animals of almost life-sized proportions competed for attention with child-scale but perfectly workable luxury cars. In each place, the air-conditioning was very welcome and their fellow shop-

pers, or window-shoppers, were often more interesting
than the wares on display.

A very frivolous morning, really. 'But after four and
a half weeks of mumps. . .' Anthony began. He didn't
need to finish the sentence.

Too soon it was lunchtime and somehow the glamour
of the Plaza Hotel or Central Park's Tavern on the
Green didn't beckon at all. Instead, heading back
towards the West Side, they found an unpretentious-
looking vegetarian restaurant on Fifty-seventh Street,
where freshly made gazpacho, crusty wholemeal bread,
a salad full of sprouts and greens and a baked loaf of
spinach and seasoned brown rice satisfied two appetites
that had had quite enough of expensive meals and rich
cream sauces.

'When I first saw that the officers' mess often got the
spare smoked salmon and *filet mignon*, I thought I was
in culinary heaven,' Anthony confessed. 'But now. . .'

'I know,' Jennie laughed. 'If I dream about food
these days, it's my mother's Scotch broth or the pot-
luck macaroni cheese she often makes on Sunday
nights.'

'In that case, we'd better make sure we finish in time
to buy your muesli and yoghurt,' he answered.

He was right, of course. Time was getting on. But
she couldn't help being disappointed all the same. It
was so nice here, anonymous in the restaurant, just the
two of them. She had half hoped that he would ask
about her mother and her family — her father and two
younger brothers, all in Dumfries — after what she had
just said about those simple, homey meals, but he
didn't.

He didn't want to. She could see that. Since the night
of her revelations to him about Ralph, herself, and Sir
Peter Farrow's death, he had carefully avoided any too
personal subjects. Having unburdened herself to him

so completely, Jennie would have liked to talk about it all a little more, to tell him that his support and her outpouring had helped. Helped a lot. But he seemed so evidently afraid of something like this. He filled too many of the spaces in their conversations with small talk.

Looking at him now, the way he was studying their bill far too intently, his dark head bent over it and a heavy frown creasing the high, square brow that she often longed to smooth or kiss, Jennie suddenly realised why. He's afraid that I'll want the same from him. A confession. A revelation. A breaking down.

And of course by this time, loving him as she now did, she did want to know what it was that had driven him from England and from a meteoric career.

'Added it up properly, have they?' she asked him gently, resigned to the fact that she had to respect his need for privacy.

'I'd say so.'

A few minutes later, they had left the restaurant.

The grocery bags were heavy by the time the *Leeward*, so closely moored against its long pier, loomed into view. Anthony had persuaded her that the pre-packaged varieties of muesli available in the super-market were entirely inadequate and had suggested that they buy ingredients to make up a large batch and share it between them. It was a good idea, but it now meant carrying bags filled with oats, wheat bran, dried fruit and nuts of several kinds, and other exotically healthy substances that the senior doctor had tracked down at three different stores. With his stationery and toiletry supplies as well, including toothpaste, shaving cream and shampoo, they were both rather burdened.

'Not far to go now,' Jennie said cheerfully as they entered the passenger terminal building. 'But these plastic handles do cut into your palms, don't they?'

Anthony Gray wasn't listening. 'My God, it *can't* be! It certainly looks like him. . . It *is*! Stephen! Stephen!' He broke into a loping run and soon caught the attention of the older couple he had seen walking towards the passengers' customs and ticket checkpoint.

By the time Jennie caught up to them, the threesome had exchanged warm greetings and were immersed in conversation. She felt a little uncertain about what to do. Join the group? Or veer off quietly and unobtrusively in the direction of the crew checkpoint? The decision was taken out of her hands.

'My dear, we've stolen your escort. Forgive us!' called a woman with prettily waved silver-grey hair.

'I think he went of his own free will,' Jennie laughed, thankful that the approach had been made so easy for her.

Clearly, these people were close friends of Anthony's and somehow it made her very happy to see him like this, part of a group, his face relaxed, casually accepting the older woman's almost maternal touch. Maternal. . . These couldn't be his parents, could they? No, this woman looked far too practical and sensible to sign herself 'Mummy' and write on shell-pink paper. . .

'Jennie, I'd like you to meet my very good friends, Stephen and Lesley Greer,' Anthony came in now, settling the question once and for all. 'They're actually taking the cruise this week. Didn't deign to let me know in advance that they'd be coming, though, for which I might not forgive them!'

'I'm pleased to meet you. Anthony has told me quite a bit about you,' Jennie smiled.

'Oh, he has, has he?' Stephen Greer beamed back, clearly very pleased at this. 'Most of it good, I hope.'

'As good as you can get!'

The sort of silly thing one said on meeting friends of a friend, but Anthony's face had darkened briefly in a

frown. It was like a cloud passing unexpectedly over
the sun and chilling the skin, and all of them felt it.

Jennie said quickly, 'Well, I must get these parcels
stowed away. And we have supplies coming on board
today, don't we, Dr Gray?'

'Yes. If you and Tilly could get them checked off our
requisitions list and unpacked before we sail. . .'

'Of course.'

'I told her you'd be fronting up by half-past two.'

'I'd better get a move on, then. We're running a bit
late.'

She hurried away to the crew check-in, but had time
to see relief in his face and relaxation return to it. What
had gone wrong? At first he had been so happy, and so
at ease.

I'll keep out of his way this week, she decided,
feeling a tenderness for him even while it was mixed
with a tinge of anger and bewilderment. Perhaps he
was afraid I'd encroach on his time alone with old
friends.

The week began uneventfully. All the supplies they
had requisitioned were accounted for and ascertained
to be in good condition. Not always the case, Jennie
had learned when unpacking and checking their previous delivery with Tilly.

On the air-conditioned ship, she soon forgot how hot
and humid the city had seemed, and although she didn't
manage to get up on deck as they sailed out of the
harbour it gave her an unselfish pleasure to think of the
passengers enjoying a perfect blue sky and a fresh but
balmy sea breeze.

She particularly enjoyed thinking about Mr and Mrs
Greer, and since Anthony hadn't put in an appearance
by quarter-past five she hoped that the three of them
were enjoying an open-air fruit cocktail together.

He came in finally at half-past five, while Jennie was

temporarily alone. Their two remaining mumps patients — a young Greek deckhand and an Indian waiter — would be well enough for discharge on Monday or Tuesday and no longer required much care, but there were still certain routine duties and Tilly was in Ward Two now, taking some time to chat. She would be off work after this until tomorrow at ten.

'Hi!' Anthony said. 'No patients yet?'

'Not yet.' It was unusual to receive anyone so early in the first day's surgery hours, but occasionally it did happen. Jennie saw that Anthony looked very relaxed and contented, and ventured to say, 'Are Mr and Mrs Greer impressed with our ship?'

'Of course! We had a drink up on deck and listened to the band. It's months since I had a chance to be up there as we sailed out. Glorious!'

'It is, isn't it? I'll never forget my first experience of it.'

'It was a complete surprise to see them in that terminal today,' he said. 'I still haven't quite forgiven them for not letting me know.'

'Don't you like surprises?' she teased, thinking how much the tinge of fresh pink buffeted into his cheeks by the breeze suited him and brightened a face that was sculptural in its good looks but too often shadowed and serious.

He smiled his slow, full smile, and that made his face even handsomer than before. 'I love surprises. . .but sometimes being able to anticipate a pleasure is even better. Now I'm far too full of plans for what they should do, and what I'll find time to do with them. We'll never fit it all in.'

'You're due for some extra time off.'

'Unfortunately, so is everybody else.'

'Hector won't begrudge you some extra. He's still working off his debt over *l'affaire Nicholson*.'

'I think he might just about feel that the debt has been paid. I ran into him on deck just now in conversation with a very attractive ——'

'Redhead?'

'Brunette. He had her positioned in a strong light and was carefully counting the crow's feet around her eyes. I'd say he won't be taking chances with anyone under a proven thirty from now on, and preferably thirty-five.'

'Hmm. . .this is a man who had sworn off women forever, I thought.'

'But you didn't believe him, did you?'

'I suppose not.'

'This one looks as though she can look after herself very well. He may be dipping into his pay packet somewhat heavily this week, because I'd say she's got her eyes on some rather expensive souvenirs that she *doesn't* intend to pay for herself!'

They both laughed, and Jennie thought again, with a small stab of painful awareness, He's happy! And it suits him so well! She added quietly and carefully aloud, 'I'm so glad your friends are here, Anthony. It's doing you good already.'

'I know,' he admitted. 'I couldn't be happier. As a doctor — and as a man — Stephen is as good as they come, and Lesley is a jewel. In many ways they've been more use to me than my own parents.'

'More use?' she probed gently. One of his too rare personal revelations. She couldn't help seizing on it, then bit her lip, hoping she hadn't just made him clam up more.

He didn't clam up. But he had misunderstood. 'Yes. Bad choice of word. I didn't mean to sound so calculating. They've been more understanding, I should have said. More supportive. They have more faith in me than I have in myself, actually.'

'But Anthony. . .' They were standing in the surgery, which wasn't large, and somehow she found herself stepping towards him and laying a hand on his upper arm then running her palm down the warm skin that was bare below the level of his short-sleeved white shirt. 'Why should you not believe in yourself? *I* believe in you! What has happened to make you doubt yourself like this, hide yourself away on a cruise ship where you hope you can't do too much damage? That's it, isn't it? That's why you're here. . .'

For a moment, she almost thought he was going to tell her. Tell her. . .or kiss her. Their eyes met. His were narrowed and searching as if, even now, he was wondering whether he could trust her. Of course you can trust me, she wanted to shout, and wanted to shake him as she shouted it. You trust the Greers, don't you? They know about it all, whatever it is, and they care about you. *I* care about you! Why can't you trust me?

His lips parted on a small sigh. 'Jennie. . .' And just the sound of her name on his lips made her grow hot with awareness.

Then Tilly emerged from Ward Two and came across the waiting-room to the surgery door, her neat tread carrying her swiftly. Unaware of the atmosphere between the English doctor and nurse, she began at once. 'Paris Nikolades is anxious about something. I think Kapil has been scaring him with stories of sterility, and with the language barrier between them the whole thing has grown out of proportion.'

'Damn! I thought we clarified the sterility issue!' Anthony bit out impatiently.

Tilly spread her hands in a gesture of helplessness. 'These rumours resurface, don't they? He is young and impressionable.'

'I'll phone up to the bridge and see if there's a Greek officer there who can be spared to come down and translate. Most of the senior officers have good English. Let's make sure we get this thing cleared up properly. I enjoy the ethnic mix among the crew, but sometimes it can create problems!'

His glance flashed briefly at Jennie and in it she read both relief and disappointment that their talk would have to remain unfinished. The disappointment—as evidenced by his impatience—was strong, but she could tell that his relief was stronger.

He's still afraid, Jennie knew suddenly. And that means he doesn't trust me enough.

Didn't trust her the way she had trusted him when she had broken down that night over four weeks ago and told him her own story. The realisation could not be a cheering one.

'I'm taking Stephen and Lesley out for the day,' Anthony said to Tilly over breakfast two days later. She had asked him about his plans.

Jennie, who was sitting in the same group, looked up in surprise. 'But I thought——'

He anticipated her objection. 'Yes, it *was* going to be tomorrow. I arranged a swap with Hector. You see, the Greers were wondering if you'd like to join us, Jennie.'

'Oh. . . I. . . I don't think so,' she answered quickly. 'I mean, I had shopping planned. I'm not in the mood for the beach.'

'Neither are they,' he persisted. 'They're not beach people. We're going to the Botanical Gardens and the Crystal Caves.'

'I really can't,' she insisted. 'I'm sorry.'

This time she didn't attempt to find an excuse, but simply picked up the breakfast tray she had finished with and left the table. She was angry with Anthony. He didn't want her to go out with them today. She could perceive this easily. It was actually frightening how sensitive she was these days to the nuances of his mood. Her excuses had been weak, she knew, but in front of Tilly and one or two others his persistence had been embarrassing.

She was alone in her cabin a few minutes later, not knowing now how to spend her day enjoyably, when he knocked at the door.

'Why did you say you were shopping today?' he demanded angrily at once when she opened it. 'I know you're not. You told me you got everything in New York.'

'Why did *you* refuse to accept a convenient excuse?' she retorted, fully matching his mood. He looked quite threatening standing there. Tall, strong-shouldered, darkly brooding. 'You don't want me with you and the Greers today. I could see it, and I was offering you a way out.'

There was a second's pause, then an explosive, 'Nonsense! Of course we want you, or we wouldn't have asked.'

She let him get away with it. Presumably, the Greers *did* want her. As an invitation made out of mere politeness, it would have been unnecessary. But *he* didn't. She was as sure of this as ever, and yet she said, 'All right. Since you've already made plans. I haven't been to the caves yet, and the Botanical Gardens are always nice.'

'Can you be ready in half an hour?' he asked woodenly.

'Easily.'

'We'll take a taxi. With four of us, there's no sense messing with scooters or buses.'

'Shall I meet you by the gangway?'

'Sounds good.'

She had little to do but wait during the next half-hour. Already dressed in well-tailored taupe linen-look shorts and a co-ordinating blouse in an abstract pattern, she did not need to change, and it took only five minutes to pack a small carrier-bag with sun-block cream, hairbrush, and anything else she might need.

The Greers were already waiting at the gangway when she arrived there, and they looked relaxed and full of anticipation about their first day ashore in Bermuda. The weather, which had been distinctly uncooperative for last week's holidaymakers, was glorious too. Anthony joined them a few minutes later and a taxi was easy to find. Soon they had reached the Botanical Gardens, after a drive in which the Greers declared that they loved Bermuda already.

'That's the hospital just up there,' Anthony told Stephen Greer. 'We have some contact with it, of course.'

And this precipitated a medical discussion between the two men that soon left them trailing behind Jennie and Mrs Greer, entirely oblivious to the sights of the gardens.

'This is *gorgeous*!' the latter said, not oblivious at all. 'Tropical plants are so *fecund*, aren't they?'

It was an unusual word to use in conversation, but Jennie was already beginning to realise that Lesley Greer was an unusual woman. With four grown-up children now, she seemed to compete with her busy husband in leading as full a life as possible.

'Now, tell me about life as a nurse on a cruise ship. I was a nurse before we had children, and I always thought it sounded like a terribly glamorous place of work. Now, *is* it? Or was that just a fantasy?'

'It is and it isn't,' Jennie laughed, and went on to give a vivid sketch of the highs and lows of her life aboard the *Leeward*.

'Have you been doing it for long?'

'Four months,' Jennie answered after a quick mental

tally. This meant that her contracted time was two-thirds through. Two more months on the *Leeward* unless she decided to renew. . .and Anthony Gray's second nine-month contract was due to expire just over a month after that.

'Do you think you'll stay long in the life?' Lesley wanted to know. Somehow, her interest was so zestful that it didn't seem too personal or prying.

'No. . .' It came out on an unintended sigh. 'It's an interlude, really.'

'Yes, it's not a life that lends itself to permanence,' Lesley agreed. 'Especially for anyone with ambition, either professional or personal. You couldn't possibly combine such a job with marrying and starting a family.'

'No, you couldn't. Many of the crew members, particularly the ship's officers, do have families, but of course they have to leave them behind. That's a sailor's life. But I couldn't do it.'

There was a small silence. They had no particular plan in their wanderings, but had come upon a grove of varied and unusually shaped palms which Lesley touched and examined absently as she passed them, a resolute figure in her lightweight khaki trousers and bright vermilion blouse.

Now she said, 'Anthony seems so much better than when we last saw him. Is he still having any trouble?'

'With. . .?'

'With the headaches, I mean, of course. I knew he wouldn't allow himself to practise medicine if he hadn't conquered the rest of it.'

She thinks I know all about it, Jennie realised. She must think that Anthony and I are very close. Perhaps even that we. . . 'He gets them very occasionally,' she answered firmly aloud.

Should she admit that she *didn't* know as much about Anthony and his past as the Greers were clearly assuming? I think Lesley hopes that we *are* involved, she thought. That's. . .touching. It hurt, too, of course.

'It seems to upset him a lot when he does,' she said to Lesley.

'Oh, yes, horribly! But he doesn't get them daily, almost constantly, the way he used to?'

'*Daily*? No!'

Jennie had only seen Anthony with a migraine headache twice. Once that first day aboard the *Leeward* and once two weeks ago at the height of the mumps outbreak when another patient had come in suffering bad lacerations after a fall on to broken glass. Surgery on the lacerations had taken two hours, and the patient had been tense and uncooperative. Not an easy evening. . .

Both these headaches had clearly been devastating and debilitating, each ending in severe nausea and leaving the senior doctor visibly drained for an hour or more afterwards. Jennie couldn't imagine what it would be like to suffer such headaches daily.

'Weekly, then?' Lesley Greer was asking.

'No, not even that. Only twice in four months, to my knowledge.'

'Thank goodness! That's marvellous!'

'He works very hard at preventing them. Spends as much time up on deck as he can, in the fresh air, watching the sea. Plays a little reed flute at night sometimes. A delightful sound. He says it relaxes him.'

This was terrible. She was digging herself in deeper by the minute, going out of her way, almost, to let Mrs Greer think that she *was* someone special in Anthony's life. Too late now to admit the truth: that they were friends, but it was a very fragile and careful relationship, and she wanted so much more.

'He's worked so hard to conquer so much,' Lesley was saying now. 'He persisted for far too long at the most intensive level of neonatal surgery. When he dropped out, Stephen did everything he could to make him understand that it wasn't a failure or an admission of weakness, but I think it's only now that Anthony might be starting to accept the truth of that.'

'I think you're right,' Jennie agreed quietly.

'He won't unburden himself, that's the trouble. You should be very glad he has a friend like my husband!'

'Oh, I. . . I am!' Jennie felt her false position once again.

'Stephen has a job to offer him. That's partly why we've come, to talk about it personally, not just through letters or the phone. It's a research position, but there will be a lot of ongoing patient contact, which I think Anthony needs. The project will last for years, following up on children who have undergone certain kinds of surgery or other invasive, aggressive medical treatment as tiny babies, to try and gauge the long-term dangers and benefits, both medically and psychologically. With his ability, and his background in surgery, Anthony is ideal. . . But do you think he's ready to go back to London?'

'I don't know.' This, at last, was nothing more nor less than the truth. 'I'm sorry. I just don't know,' she repeated.

'Don't you?' Lesley Greer's disappointment was evident. 'I suppose I'll just have to leave it to Stephen and Anthony themselves, and trust that the right thing will happen. I wonder if they're talking about it now?'

She looked around and saw the two men walking absently back and forth among a lay-out of rose bushes that looked rather bedraggled and heat-weary at this time of year. They were clearly immersed in a very intense discussion. 'I don't want to interrupt. . .' Lesley said, frowning.

'We haven't seen the greenhouses yet,' Jennie pointed out.

'Good idea. They'll see us heading up that way and can join us later, when they're ready.'

If the sea-water at Bermuda's beaches seemed clear and magical, the water in the Crystal Caves seemed a hundred times more so. With Anthony beside her and the Greers some distance off on the other side of the guided tour group, Jennie watched it, mesmerised by the play of the cave's artfully placed lights on the surface, and by the shadings of green to blue which told her that in places the water was far deeper than it looked.

In the background came the female cave guide's voice, with the lilting half-English, half-something-else accent of the native Bermudian. Jennie had stopped listening. She might miss out on a speleological fact or two, but somehow the cave's beauty seemed more important than its history and geology today.

'I hate to bother you with this,' Anthony came in, seeming as reluctant as Jennie was to break the mood with conversation. 'But somehow Stephen and Lesley have got hold of a misconception about us and I think you should know about it.'

'Yes. . .' She knew what was coming.

'They think there's a romance going on. Sorry. I guess they assumed on Saturday when they first saw us. . .'

'It doesn't matter,' she came in quickly. 'After all, we *are* friends. I'm not embarrassed. Don't worry.'

Friends. A ludicrous understatement, really, in view of how she actually felt about him. Now, for instance, she was acutely conscious of his height, his warmth, his nearness, that full upper lip and those dark, smoky eyes. In a patch of dimmer light several yards off, she saw a honeymoon couple touch and kiss, which made her long to do the same.

'I'll find a way to tell them the truth,' Anthony was saying.

'You may disappoint them,' she answered lightly.

He smiled. 'I may disappoint them in something that's closer to their hearts than that.'

'You mean Stephen Greer has spoken to you about the research position with him in London and you're not going to take it?' The drama of the cave made her bold in speech.

'Lesley mentioned it to you at the gardens, I suppose. . . I haven't decided yet, but yes, as you say, I'm probably going to turn it down. I'll renew my contract with the shipping company for another nine months.'

Still running away! Nearly four months ago, she had told him it was the right thing, but. . . How bad could that past of his be? Not bad enough to earn condemnation from the Greers. Not bad enough to destroy Jennie's intuitive trust. Anthony's own faith, it seemed, was the one thing that was lacking. Couldn't he find a way to get it back? Did he have to struggle with the issue entirely alone?

And suddenly, thinking of this stubbornness in him, she was so angry that the words hissed from her mouth with an almost primeval surge. 'Sometimes I think you're a complete fool, Anthony Gray!'

CHAPTER NINE

ANGER. It set the tone for the rest of the week. The happy relaxation that the Greers had at first brought to Anthony seemed to have gone, at least when Jennie saw him in the ship's hospital. Instead, he was brooding, taciturn and distant. Fortunately, it was a quiet week, with their last mumps patients discharged and very little emergency on-call time.

Anthony must have been successful in letting the Greers know that there was no romantic involvement between Jennie and himself, the former decided, as she was not invited again to participate in their outings, meals or cocktail hours, as she had half expected to be.

She met up with Lesley Greer by chance in the lift on the last afternoon of the cruise and was greeted warmly, though.

'It has been a marvellous week!' the older woman said, sounding quite sincere. 'The ship is gorgeous. . . I almost feel she's *mine* but I'm sure everyone feels that. And Bermuda seemed like a paradise. If I'd known about the place thirty years ago, I would have done my best to marry a Bermudian!'

So perhaps Anthony's mood had been different while he was with his old friends. Not surprising, perhaps. After all, it was Jennie who had called him a fool! And she *meant* it, too! she insisted to herself more than once over the rest of the week — even though, unfortunately, it didn't do a thing to quench the wistful thirsting of her love.

That Friday night, though, just as evening surgery hours were winding down, anger set the tone once again, and this time Jennie was not involved at all. Stephen had come down for a tour of their facilities and, Jennie somehow guessed, to thrash out once and for all the question of the research position in England. He wanted Anthony's final decision.

Jennie should have been able to leave with the last patient, and no doubt the two doctors closeted in the surgery — with the door standing just slightly ajar — thought that she had. But in fact she was too worried to leave. There was a discrepancy between her tally of a certain drug and the tally as it should be according to the records. Not a serious discrepancy, and not a very dangerous drug, but, in view of the shipping company's insistence on scrupulous accuracy in such matters, a worrisome occurrence none the less. They were always so careful. How could it have happened? She set about trying to find out. . .

And heard everything that happened between Stephen Greer and Anthony Gray. The conversation started amicably enough, and Jennie was not distracted from her careful entry-by-entry study of the dispensary books. Evidently, Stephen Greer was still confident that Anthony would accept the job in the end.

But soon he grew impatient and his voice was raised.

'Damn it! What are you afraid of in yourself?'

'You know very well, Stephen,' was Anthony's quieter reply.

'But you've said youself it's conquered. No, Anthony, it's *not* that. You think you're weak, don't you? Too weak to take on anything stressful or difficult.'

'Isn't there ample evidence that that's true?' Again, the ship's doctor was controlled and quiet.

'No, there *isn't*! There's every evidence to the contrary. You persisted in neonatal surgery for four years when the personal toll it was taking on you would have pushed a lesser man out after four months. And then, when a lesser man would have accepted the sinecure your father was offering you in that practice of his. . . Tell me! Do most of his patients still spend more money on their poodles than some people can afford to spend on a family of ten children?'

There was a rather bleak laugh. 'I'm afraid so.'

'But you couldn't bring yourself to work in a practice that catered to London's wealthy hypochondriac population, even for a well-earned six months of ease. No! You had to go into the front line, the opposite extreme, working a hundred-and-twenty hour weeks with homeless people, drug addicts, indigents of every kind.'

'And look what happened to me. . .'

'And look what you *did*. You *saw* that it was happening to you and got out before it was too late. Got out of medicine altogether until you felt you could practise again without risk. Do you think a lesser man would have done that? No! A lesser man, a lesser doctor, would have been on the streets or in prison by now.'

'I still get headaches, Stephen.'

'Occasionally. Very occasionally. You'll always get them,' the older doctor acknowledged bluntly.

In the dispensary, Jennie put her finger on an entry in the records that she couldn't quite read. It was in Hector's writing, hastily scribbled, and it dated from the height of their recent mumps epidemic. This *could* be the problem. On a nearby pad, she made a note of it and kept looking.

'But you know how to handle the headaches now,' Stephen Greer was saying in the surgery. 'You've told me yourself that you have half a dozen relaxation techniques at your disposal, from flute-playing to deep breathing, and you've told me that they work, ninety-five per cent of the time.'

'And the other five per cent? You say the research position won't be stressful. . .'

'It won't be. That's the beauty of it. No on-call or emergency work. There'll be a lot to do, but you can take it at your own pace. Important, cutting-edge, satisfying medicine. That's the beauty of it, Anthony,' he repeated. 'And I *want* you for it! Damn it, you're too good!'

'I'm also very stubborn,' came the quiet reply. 'There's still something missing, something I need in order to be a hundred per cent sure that things can't go wrong again.'

'A hundred per cent! That's your trouble. . .and one of your greatest assets. One of the reasons why I want you. Your work and your thoroughness will be a hundred per cent as well.'

'And until I find out what that missing thing is, and add it to my life, I can't go back.'

A heavy silence fell after this last, very final pronouncement. Jennie came to the end of the records she was searching. Nothing else had leapt out at her as being a possible error. She decided to ask Hector about it at once. There was a good chance that he would be in his cabin getting ready for an evening in the casino with Brittany, the attractive older brunette he had been raving about this week. She picked up the phone.

'That's your final answer, isn't it?' she heard Stephen Greer say in the surgery as she listened to the burring ring.

'Yes.'

'Well, you've got three months to change your mind. I'll sound out some other prospects but won't make any definite offers until that three months is up. But I *can't* hold off any longer than that. The project gets under way in four months.'

'Do what's best for the project, Stephen.'

'Ha! You won't let me do that!'

'I meant —— '

'I know what you meant.'

'It's only fair to tell you. . . I've just written a letter to the shipping company today, indicating that I'll renew my contract again when the time comes.'

There was an air of resignation and stubbornness in both of them that made each deep voice, normally confident and brisk, sound tired and heavy. Jennie realised that she had been hanging on the phone for far too long. Hector must already have gone out. Or perhaps he was eating with Brittany in the passengers' dining-room tonight. She was just about to hang up when there was a clatter at the other end and Hector's voice came hurriedly. 'Hello?'

'Hector?'

'Oh, it's you, Jennie. Sorry. I was in the shower and didn't hear. What is it? Not an emergency?'

'I doubt it,' she answered. 'Just a discrepancy in the dispensary records that I'm trying to clear up. I've found an entry in your writing that I might have mis-read. . .or you might have miswritten. Can you possibly remember?'

Out of the corner of her eye she saw the two doctors emerge from the surgery and gave them a brief wave. They were clearly taken aback to find that she was still here. 'It dates from the worst night of our mumps crisis,' she explained to Hector.

'That terrible Thursday? When in addition we had the road crash, the sunburn, the yeast infections, the. . .'

'And the laceration case, yes, that's the night.'

'And you say there's a discrepancy?'

'Yes, in the medication supplies. We've got less of a particular analgesic than the books says we should have. And it says here. . .'

She read the entry aloud, aware that the two doctors were listening, each with an odd expression. Anthony shifted restlessly then looked at Stephen Greer, his features twisted in a mixture of guilt, anger and. . . could it be pleading?. . .that Jennie had never seen on his face before. 'Stephen. . .' he began.

'Don't—even—suggest it!' the older man hissed. 'After everything you've said and everything I know of you, do you think I'd suspect——?' He broke off, shaking his head in helpless outrage.

'My writing, is it. . .?' Hector was saying over the phone. 'I might remember. . . Can I come down and have a look? Yes, I'm almost certain, now that I think about it. I was so tired that night. Of course it should have been ten times that amount with all those patients.'

'Thank goodness! It wasn't a big thing, but we're always so careful, and it worried me. Could you come and make absolutely certain?'

'Of course. I'll be two minutes.'

Jennie replaced the phone and looked up at the two doctors. Somehow, the snatch of conversation they had overheard had renewed the tension between them, and she was anxious to assuage it. The Greers were leaving the ship tomorrow, and Anthony valued and needed their friendship so much. If this week had strained that friendship in any way, she wanted to do what she could to put things right.

'Hector,' she explained quickly. 'You probably heard. I was worried about a small discrepancy, but he's pretty certain that he's solved it. Possibly I just misread his writing when I was tallying up.'

'That sounds to me like a likely explanation,' Stephen Greer came in firmly. 'Don't you think, Anthony?'

'Yes. Of course. I'm sorry. I had no right to jump to conclusions about what you were thinking, Stephen. Bad luck, Jennie, you've had to stay late over it.'

'It doesn't matter. I won't have missed staff mess dinner. You two go. I'll lock up.'

The two men left, Hector soon confirmed the solution to the discrepancy once and for all, and Jennie was left with more questions about Anthony Gray than ever. . .

'So you've definitely decided not to renew your contract, Jennie?'

'Yes,' she nodded, trying to put on a bright face. 'I sent out my resignation today with the ship's mail.'

It was a month now since the Greers had left the *Leeward*, and relations between the senior doctor and his English nurse had been very amicable in that time. He seemed to have forgiven her for calling him a fool. Heaven knew, she had tried to show him that she no longer thought so. . .if she ever really had.

The heated exchange she had overheard between Anthony and Stephen Greer had told her very clearly that there was more to him and his past than she could know, and somehow she found herself siding with Anthony now, and not with the older man. Dr Gray seemed to know what he needed, what he was capable of, and no one else could dispute that. Stephen Greer — and Jennie herself — might be impatient with the man's thoroughness in conquering his own past, but Anthony was right. He could not go back until *he* believed that he was ready.

That was not the reasoning of a fool. Several times, in fact, she had been on the point of apologising for her angry use of the word, but the moment had never seemed right, and now she thought it best to let it lie. . .

'Congratulations, Jennie,' Anthony was saying. They were together in the hospital, preparing to open up for evening hours on a Saturday, the first day of the cruise week and almost always a quiet one.

'For what?'

'For overcoming your demons.'

'Oh, Anthony! They weren't very bad ones. Talking to you about it that night told me so. I just needed the distance and time to get it all in proportion. Now, when I think about it, it's just, Thank goodness I didn't marry Ralph! And I think that what happened with Sir Peter Farrow, although I can believe now that it *wasn't* my fault, has ultimately made me a better nurse. I've really learnt that nothing in medicine is ever routine, and it can be dangerous even to use the word.'

'There you are. That's all cause for congratulation, isn't it?'

'All right,' she laughed. 'Yes, it is. Compared to what I felt five months ago.'

'And you'll return to. . .what?'

'I don't know,' she admitted. 'My family for a month or two, I think. Then I'm not quite sure what, or even where. That's the great thing about nursing. So many choices. Frankly, the *Leeward* is so much its own little world that it's difficult to think about the future in a concrete way.'

'Frankly', she had said, but she wasn't actually being frank at all. Her reluctance to commit herself to a definite future had far more to do with Anthony Gray himself than she could possibly admit to him. She *did* want to stay with her family for a while, but she also wanted to leave herself free in case Anthony. . .

Stupid! Hopeless! she told herself, to no avail.

'Sounds very understandable,' he commented on her last words.

A faint sensation of movement and sound made them both aware that the *Leeward* had pulled out from her moorings and was under way. Time to stop chatting and see to more of the inevitable paperwork that seemed to generate itself entirely independently of patients. Anthony began to tidy his desk, and Jennie caught sight of some pale pink stationery among his pile of mail.

'News from your family?' she ventured lightly.

'How did you know?'

'I recognised your mother's writing paper.' She gestured at the envelope that had slipped to one side, and the two flimsy sheets beneath it.

He glanced down. 'Oh. . .' With a sudden, angry gesture he had swept up letter and envelope, crushing them together in a tight ball and tossing them into a nearby waste-paper basket. Jennie was too stunned at his action to speak or move, and he seemed momentarily frozen as well. Then, slowly, he leaned down to the basket, retrieved the pink sheets and smoothed them out again.

'I shouldn't have done that,' he said soberly. 'Childish! But satisfying. It expressed what I felt. I'll have to write it to her instead: Please stop pestering me to go into practice with my father in every letter that you write. Whatever else I may do with my life and my career, it's *not* going to be that, and your veiled putdowns and odious comparisons with my elder brother will not change anything.'

'Anthony. . .'

'No, it's time I learned to laugh about it. . .or to be openly angry.'

'Instead of bottling it up?'

'Yes.'

'Actually, I think you've been getting very good at *not* bottling,' she told him sincerely.

'You mean that day when we hiked along the railway trail. . .'

'And I dropped a rock on your foot? Yes.'

'Rock? I seem to remember you had decided it was a valuable fossil.'

She remembered the occasion two weeks ago and laughed at the image of him swearing at her — mild words, but used with a force and thoroughness that cleared the air almost immediately.

'Well, those muddy marks on it looked like fossilised creatures at first,' she returned sheepishly, 'and when I passed it across to you to have a look, I didn't realise you hadn't got hold of it properly yet.'

'Just do me one favour, Jennie,' was his response, so serious that for a moment she was quite alarmed.

'Y-yes?'

'Promise me that you won't *ever* give up nursing and take up palaeontology!'

Having strayed off the subject, they didn't talk any more about his mother's letter, and it really was time to get down to work. But the light-hearted ending to what had started off as a serious discussion reminded Jennie of other outings they had taken together lately. Somehow, without it seeming a particularly momentous thing, they had fallen into the habit of spending most of their time off in Bermuda together.

Sometimes they went to the beach, sometimes for a pleasant waterfront lunch somewhere. Sometimes they decided on a more ambitious excursion, like the day he had mentioned, when they had hiked along a section of Bermuda's old abandoned railway-line, now opened up as a scenic walking trail.

Special moments from these times stood out in Jennie's memory: the day he had climbed a rocky outcrop on the shore 'just because it's there', as he had said. Clad only in shorts and a cotton T-shirt, he had looked impossibly capable and athletic swarming up the rough face, with hands gripping easily on to each knob of rock. Then there was the day they had hiked a different section of the railway trail and had found an injured bird.

This time, her memory was of the gentleness of his hands, not of their strength, as he had tried to warm the tiny ball of feathers between his cupped palms. Too late, though. The bird must have been struggling on the ground for some time before they found it, and after several minutes it died.

'We won't bury it,' he'd said. 'That seems too sentimental, don't you think?'

'And we don't have a thing to dig with.'

'But let's find a hollow spot where we can cover it with leaves so it can. . .I don't know. . .it sounds stupid, but. . .decompose with dignity.'

They had both laughed in spite of themselves at his choice of words, then had done as he suggested and laid the little creature to rest. . .

Silly things to remember, perhaps, but somehow the images were very vivid and Jennie knew that they would stay with her always. But there was one image that she could not add to her store of memories from this time — his kiss. . .because it had never been more clear to her than over these past few weeks that all he wanted was friendship.

These were always daytime outings, never at night, never with the added magic of moonlight and hazy blue darkness that night-time brought, and she knew it was deliberate on his part. He remembered their first evening together five months ago, and didn't want to run any such risk again.

Sensibly, she knew she should be glad of the fact that they so rarely touched, because it was always his touch that made her fully realise her love. But the wilful, sensual part of her, which only seemed to be growing stronger, wanted his kisses anyway, even if they could seal no shared future.

* * *

'Yes, I'm sorry. You're definitely in labour,' Anthony Gray said to a very anxious woman three hours later. 'Your cervix is already three centimetres dilated.'

'Isn't there some drug you can give her to stop it?' the woman's fair-haired husband came in anxiously. They were both in their mid-to-late thirties, this was their first child. . .and it shouldn't, according to her dates, be making an appearance for another eight weeks.

'I'm afraid not,' the doctor said. 'Did you feel that warm bath of fluid gushing out as I began to examine you?'

'Yes, I did. I wasn't sure. . .'

'It was your membrane rupturing. Even if we *could* halt the progress of your labour at this stage it would be too dangerous. Your baby needs that fluid-filled amniotic sac until labour, and it needs the membrane to be intact to keep out infection.'

'Then. . .we're only a few hours out of New York. Can the ship turn back?' the husband wanted to know.

'I'm afraid not.'

'I've been such an idiot.' The dark-haired woman sobbed suddenly, her wide mouth trembling uncontrollably. 'I felt some contractions while we were waiting in the passenger terminal to board, but I've been so looking forward to this cruise. Our last vacation before the baby comes. I didn't want to cancel it. The contractions weren't painful. I thought they were just stronger versions of those Braxton-Hicks things I've been having over the past two weeks.'

'Your doctor hadn't seen any unusual signs last week when he examined you?'

'No, he was quite happy to write out the medical certificate that the shipping company requires, saying I was fit to travel.'

'She has none of the risk indicators for prematurity,

and no family history of it,' the husband came in earnestly, as if stressing this would somehow make the labour miraculously stop.

As he spoke, his wife was gripped by another contraction, more painful than the previous one and ten minutes after it.

'Jennie, make them comfortable in Ward Three, would you? Wards One and Two are empty as well,' Anthony explained to the couple, 'but they're closer to the waiting-room and I want you to have some privacy.'

Wards Four and Five were even more private, Jennie knew, but the hospital's small and infrequently-used morgue was directly opposite and Mrs Astwood didn't need any reminder that their tiny baby might not survive long enough to reach a humidicrib and special-care nursery at Bermuda's King Edward Memorial Hospital.

She settled the couple into their room and then stayed with Mrs Astwood while her husband went to fetch some personal items from their cabin. Another contraction came, and the mother-to-be began the breathing exercises she had learnt at a natural-child-birth class only the week before.

'Did I do that right?' she asked Jennie when the pain of the contraction had ebbed away. But her smile was forced.

'It looked good,' Jennie answered. 'You'll find it easier once Mr Astwood comes back, too.'

'I know. He's so supportive. . .'

He returned a few minutes later, bringing everything she could possibly need—a hairbrush, lemon drops to suck on, lipsalve in case her mouth felt dry.

'They told us in the class to bring tennis-balls,' he said helplessly. 'But I didn't have any. And I forget what they were for. . .'

'To press into my lower back if I have back pain,' his

wife said. Her brow was dewy now, dampening the straight dark hair that Jennie had helped her to pull back out of the way into a neat ponytail.

Clearly Mr and Mrs Astwood were the kind of couple who took the birth experience very seriously, and it seemed so unfair that they should be overtaken by something as potentially tragic as this. In the days before humidicribs and neonatal intensive care, many babies born at thirty-two weeks' gestation *had* survived, but many had not. This baby's first twenty-four hours of life here on the *Leeward* would be critical.

Leaving the couple alone, Jennie went to the surgery where Anthony was pacing to and fro, deep in thought. She hesitated before interrupting him, seeing the telltale frown on his brow, which she so often longed to smooth, but he saw her and for a while the frown cleared.

'All settled in?'

'Yes.'

'I'll come and see her in a minute. This is going to be a long night.' The cheerfulness was forced.

'She's lying down. Should I encourage her to walk? I know that's supposed to speed things up. Is that what we want?'

'You mean, do we hold that baby back until we get to Bermuda, if we can?'

'Yes.'

'Jennie, that's thirty-six hours. A long labour is stressful for the baby as well as for the mother,' he answered heavily. 'This baby is small. It's going to slide easily through the birth canal and it's probably going to be born quickly. Whether she stands or lies down won't make a lot of difference. If it brings her more comfort and seems to push things along, get her to walk around.'

He began pacing again.

'Anthony, are you —— ?'

'No,' he returned, anticipating the soothing enquiry she was about to make. 'Of course I'm not all right! I've seen premature babies before, remember? A lot of them! I've seen them struggling for life and losing the struggle even with the most intensive level of modern care. And we haven't got that here. I need to make sure I've thought of the best substitutes.'

'In a way,' she said slowly, 'it would be easier if we *weren't* docking in Burmuda on Monday morning, wouldn't it? Then we'd know it was all up to us.'

'Yes,' he agreed. 'This way, there's a window of time in which we just have to keep that baby alive so it can get to KEMH. We'll do it, too! I'm *determined* we'll do it!'

Five hours passed and it was after midnight. All the preparations that Anthony had planned were already made. Mrs Astwood's contractions were steady and increasing in intensity and frequency, and she had reached six centimetres of dilation. Although both doctor and nurse checked on the couple regularly, they knew that privacy during the intense work of labour was important, too. While Mr and Mrs Astwood breathed together through each contraction and rested between them, Anthony and Jennie could only wait.

He sent her out for a meal at eight-thirty, but waved away her suggestion that he go himself as soon as she got back.

'I had a late lunch,' he said. 'I'm not hungry,' and she didn't dare to insist, although she wanted to.

'I think she'll soon hit transition phase,' Jennie reported to Anthony at a quarter to one. 'Her husband is having to work much harder now to keep her on track with the breathing and relaxation.'

Relaxation. . . She stopped and looked at the doctor, who sat behind his desk in the surgery, frowning over a medical journal. There was a tell-tale familiarity in the drawn pallor of his face, and suddenly she knew that the signs of mounting strain in him were caused by more than just Mrs Astwood's premature labour.

'You've got a headache, haven't you?' she said to him quietly.

'Yes.'

'Since when?'

'This afternoon. I could have fought it off, but with the Astwoods and their problem. . .'

'It only got worse,' she finished for him. 'Go up on deck, Anthony. You've got time, and I can page you as soon as you're needed. Fresh air always helps, doesn't it?'

'It's gone beyond that. You were right. I should have eaten.'

'Then for heaven's sake *take* something for it! That dispensary of ours is a pill-lover's heaven, but you treat even aspirin as if it were poisonous.'

He looked up at her. 'Jennie, for me it *is* poisonous!'

'What do you mean?' she whispered. There was an intensity to his gaze that alarmed her.

'I have to tell you, don't I? I probably should have told you months ago, but I've been so determined to keep things. . .' He didn't finish.

'Yes, do tell me,' she said quietly, coming up to him at the desk. 'Tell me the whole thing. And while you do I'm going to massage your head and your shoulders and your neck, and I want you to close your eyes and forget all about the Astwoods. . .'

She came behind him and reached around to unbutton the top two buttons of his shirt so that she could pull its collar aside and reach the bare, warm skin of his shoulder and neck muscles with her hands. Beginning with light, stroking movements from the top of his head down to the firm webbing of muscle and sinew above his shoulderblades, she didn't speak, and at first she thought that he wasn't going to either.

She had shut the surgery door when she came in and it was very quiet in here. Quiet, and lit only by a yellow-hued desk lamp. His hair felt glossy and clean, his neck warm, and his shoulders tight with tension. Even the muscles at his temples and on his face were knotted, she found, but her fingers seemed to find the tight spots by instinct as she worked to smooth them away.

'I've always been prone to headaches,' he began at last. 'Even as a child. My mother took me to a whole circus of specialists, but they could find nothing definitively wrong. A muscle convergence problem in my eyes, one of them said. Stress, said another. Eye-strain from reading and watching computer screens in the lab at school, said a third. It was finally decided that all three things were partially to blame, as well as other possible factors that they couldn't even guess at. Allergies? Something in the structure of the bone around my eyes and temples? They told my parents that medicine was out of the question as a career. Too stressful. Too much reading. But I was determined and so were my mother and father. My brother Edmund, who is six years older than I am, was already leaving a blazing trail of success in his medical studies.'

'Your brother,' Jennie came in. 'The one with whom you are "odiously" compared?'

'That's the one. . . So I went ahead. I've told you that part. Working with Stephen, giving it up finally. I lost a fiancée when I did so, by the way. She had been very ambitious for me. That seems a long time ago. The headaches were a factor in my dropping out, but not the major one, as you know.'

'Yes, the helplessness you told me about that first night up on deck, when you had to face suffering in a tiny child.'

'You must have heard part of my argument with Stephen in here a few weeks ago. . .?'

'Yes, part,' she admitted.

'My father has — I have to say it — a horribly cushy little practice. He wanted me to join him in a junior capacity. *Very* junior. Edmund, by this time, was a ridiculously successful orthopaedic surgeon. Still is.'

'And your parents were angry with you for dropping out of neonatal surgery?'

'Particularly my mother. She's funny about illness. When the specialists couldn't diagnose or cure the headaches, they suddenly became my own fault, a weakness. I shouldn't speak to you like this about my parents. It's disloyal.'

'Not if it's truthful. Not when I care. . .when we're friends.' There! She had almost admitted her love, just blurted it out in this atmosphere of intense, shared revelation.

'Anyway, I wouldn't join my father and instead I went to work at a clinic with indigent patients.'

'Yes, you've told me something about it,' she said, remembering the night in the passengers' dining-room when Charles M. King had come up to their table.

'What I haven't told you. . .this is the important part, Jennie. . .is about the drugs.'

'Drugs?'

'It's very simple, really. I became an addict.' The word dropped from his lips as if he hated to even say it. 'It started with prescription pain-killers for the headaches. In retrospect, in my last two years under Stephen I was already downing too many of them, but pretty mild ones at that stage. It's so easy for a doctor, though, to get access to the stronger stuff. If anything, my work at the clinic was more stressful than neonatal surgery, and I gradually began to use the more heavy-duty pills. Morphine-based. I needed them. The old ones were too mild to work any more. I began to feel marvellous when I was doped up, and like utter hell when I wasn't. Some of the patients we saw were drug addicts, of course. Heroin, cocaine, barbiturates — you name it. And addicts can be perceptive about one another. None of my fellow doctors guessed that I had a problem, but one of my patients *did*. She pointed out how inefficient pills were, how long and agonising the wait could be between when you swallowed them and when they took effect. She convinced me. . . Actually, I was so far gone that we almost became involved. My God! She convinced me to try the direct route.'

'You mean. . .?'

'Injection.'

'Anthony. . .'

'I tried it once. Once. Had the sense to use a sterile needle. But there was suddenly something so sordid about it. I'd seen enough about where it could lead. I knew I had to stop cold, get away, and I did.'

'So that was what Stephen Greer meant when he talked about your courage, and what a lesser man would have done.'

'Yes, bless him. He was the person I went to. Him and Lesley. Told them everything. Stayed with them for four weeks during the worst of the withdrawal. The headaches during that time were excruciating. They wanted me to try something safer —'

'But you wouldn't, of course. Anthony Gray, you are stubborn!'

'And still a fool?'

'No, never that! I was quite wrong!'

For a few minutes she massaged him in silence and could feel the tension draining away.

'I couldn't take any sort of medication. I didn't dare. I still don't dare, and I probably never will. Seems strange for a doctor, doesn't it?'

'Not really.'

'That road was quick and easy enough to travel down the first time. If I ever started again, it would probably be even quicker.'

'So you gave up medicine and became a stonemason?'

'Yes.'

'Couldn't you have found something a bit less— um—noisy?'

'Oddly, it helped. I needed something very physical to do, very overpowering. And every night when I came home from work I practised relaxation techniques, went for long walks in the fresh air, exercised my eyes, played the flute, and it began to work. Now, I nearly always see a headache coming and can stave it off.'

'But not tonight?'

'Not tonight.'

'Do you think your mother's letter had anything to do with it?'

'Probably. My brother is once again invoked as the ideal son. Strangely enough, he and I have always got on extremely well. You'd think we'd have been at each other's throats, wouldn't you?'

'Does he know about everything?'

'No, but I think he guesses more than my parents do. He was very supportive about my taking this job. He's a good man, Edmund. Delightful wife and children, too. Stephen and Lesley are the only ones who know the full story. . .and now you.'

'You keep your life in England very separate from your life here, don't you?' she came in quietly.

'It seems best that way, Jennie.'

'Does it?'

'Yes. Don't you think that's the last thing I need? To let anything about *this* life get too important? When I do go back to England, as I will, I don't want to be bringing any emotional baggage with me.'

'I see. . .'

If he had any understanding of how much his words meant to her, he gave no sign of it.

But he *has* to know, Jennie realised miserably. That's why he sounded so gentle just then. Perhaps my voice and words can hide it, but my hands and fingers can't. Slowly, she drew the massage to a close. 'Any better?' she said cheerfully aloud.

'Much, thanks. It's still there, but the danger of nausea is past.'

'Still, I'm going to get Room Service to bring you a very large sandwich,' she said.

'I won't argue with that.'

She turned to the phone, but before she could lift the receiver he said quietly behind her, 'Talking about it all helped too, Jennie. I thought once it was out I might regret telling you. But I don't. I want you to remember that, in spite of what I just said about emotional baggage.'

'All right. I will remember. Thanks.' It came out in bright, staccato tones that anyone would have known were not sincere.

He knows how I feel about him, and he's being. . . *kind*, she thought, half angry, half simply miserable. Turning from him, she dialled the room service extension and ordered two club sandwiches.

Moments later there was a knock at the door. 'Can you come?' Michael Astwood looked tired and frantic. 'She's in so much pain now. It can't be normal!'

But it was. Frances Astwood had reached the most intense part of labour, when contractions came thundering one on top of the other, leaving only seconds to gather strength between each one. Even as her husband returned to her, with Anthony and Jennie hurrying behind, she called frantically, 'I need to push! I have to push *now*!'

'Not yet,' said Anthony urgently. 'Pant and blow until this contraction ebbs.'

'No!' She was angry and out of control.

'Yes!' He met her gaze with equal force, but there was no time to explain that he needed to examine her one more time to make sure the cervix was completely ready. Straining against the now paper-thin tissue too early could damage it. With another contraction already beginning to grip her, the patient fought the examination but Anthony managed to slip in a gloved hand and found that indeed one part of the cervix's rim still needed to be pushed back as it had formed a sort of fold. He was able to do this with his fingers and then Mrs Astwood was free to begin the most arduous part of labour — pushing the baby out.

As far as possible, they were ready for the tiny child. During their lull in activity earlier in the evening, Jennie had prepared Ward Two next door. The heating had been raised and repeated kettles of water boiled there so that the air was moist and warm. Also, a tank of oxygen was slowly hissing out its contents into the room, to increase subtly the level of the gas that would reach the baby's immature lungs. Jennie had heated blankets in a makeshift fashion, too, wrapping them around bottles of hot water so that the infant, whose body could cool with dangerous rapidity, would be kept warm.

'Since we *haven't* got technology on our side,' Anthony had explained earlier, 'we're going to use the primitive approach to our advantage. If the baby is simply too small — and I hope that's all we'll be faced with — we'll keep it lying on its mother's belly and wheel her into the warmed room as soon as I've delivered the afterbirth and mended any tearing. We're going to try and make this as natural a transition as possible between the womb and the outside world. We'll encourage her to give the baby the breast straight away, too, but it may be too small to show much sucking reflex as yet. That could be discouraging for Mrs Astwood, and we may have to prepare an IV to prevent dehydration.'

'An IV into a premature new-born?'

'I've done it, remember? Sometimes it's hell finding a vein, but it always gets done in the end.' Grim-voiced, this.

The bed in Ward Two had been wheeled elsewhere so that Mrs Astwood and the baby could be transferred as they were, using the wheeled bed from Ward Three. Hopefully, warmth, fluid, oxygen moisture and the skin-to-skin, heart-to-heart contact with the mother would be enough to keep the fragile little life from petering out before the baby reached King Edward Memorial Hospital's special-care nursery.

It was almost time. The urgency of Mrs Astwood's pushing had increased and the baby's head, covered with black hair, had crowned. 'Reach down. Feel your baby's head,' Anthony urged, and this was enough to encourage the exhausted woman to a last burst of strength during the next contraction. The head emerged and seconds later the rest of the tiny baby had slipped free.

Actually, not so tiny. 'It's a boy!' said Anthony. And it was already breathing well, if that lusty cry was any indication. 'Mrs Astwood, the baby is perfect! Are you sure about your dates?'

'I. . . I think so. At least. . .'

'This is a thirty-six-week child, not a thirty-two, and he must weigh well over five pounds. Nearer to six, I'd say.'

'You mean. . .?' the father came in on a choked sound that was almost a sob.

'No doubt about it. This baby is going to be just fine.'

CHAPTER TEN

AN HOUR later, the drama was all over, and mother, father and baby Michael Junior were enjoying each other's company in the warm, humid atmosphere of Ward Two. Mrs Astwood had not torn during the delivery, so there were no stitches to put in, and the afterbirth had been delivered easily, the placenta complete and well-formed.

When things were calmer, Anthony had examined the baby carefully. He had used the Dubowitz scoring system, which involved assessing various physiological and neurological criteria in order to determine the exact gestational age of the baby, and this had confirmed his initial impression that Mrs Astwood's pregnancy was actually a month further advanced than she and her obstetrician had believed.

'These things do happen,' he reassured her. 'What you thought was your last period may have been a mild episode of early pregnancy bleeding. Presumably you didn't have a sonogram at any stage?'

'No,' she answered. 'My obstetrician doesn't do them as a routine thing, and everything was going so well that we didn't feel it was necessary.'

'An early sonogram would have given a clue that your dates were wrong.'

'Next time, I'll have one!'

'A lot of obstetricians have an ultrasound machine in their offices these days, and it *is* sometimes useful to know for sure. . .as in this case,' Anthony answered. 'Although, of course, everything has turned out well in spite of the mistake.'

'I was so upset and frightened,' Mrs Astwood said. 'But now that Michael is safely here it doesn't seem important at all.'

'My first baby at sea,' Jennie commented to Anthony a little later. They had left the couple alone and were drinking tea and sharing the sandwiches that the room service waiter had—with an alarmed expression— delivered during the very height of the crisis. 'Will this affect its citizenship, do you think?'

'Born in international waters, of American parents, on a Greek-owned ship? I shudder to think,' Anthony laughed. 'And I'm very happy to have done *my* part, so I can shuffle that question on to someone else! These sandwiches are good. I'll order some for the Astwoods, shall I? They didn't have dinner, of course, and both are probably starving after their hard work.'

The second lot of sandwiches was soon delivered and, reluctantly, Jennie drained the last of her tea. There was something very satisfying about sitting here with Anthony in the aftermath of a medical success and sharing a little of the glow that enveloped the new parents. She didn't want it to end, but knew that it had to.

There was no reason for herself and Anthony both to remain here all night. The baby was healthy and strong, and Mrs Astwood's uterus was contracting back into her lower abdomen as it should. Anthony could go to bed while Jennie remained, and he would be back with his patients in three minutes if she had to page him for any reason.

Slowly, she got to her feet and took their empty cups to rinse out in the sink, then made herself say it. 'Well, nothing much left for us to do now. . .'

But he seemed to be in no hurry. 'This has been a good night, hasn't it?'

'Yes, a far better outcome than we could have dared to hope for,' she answered.

'I didn't mean the Astwoods, Jennie,' was his quiet clarification. 'I meant us.'

'Us?'

'I should have talked to you about my addiction long ago.' 'My addiction'. Now he was able to say the words very naturally, Jennie noticed. That in itself was a breakthrough, and her heart went out to him. He went on, 'Once or twice I was on the point of it. . .'

'I know.'

'But. . .how can I explain?'

'You didn't trust me to trust you.'

He laughed softly. 'That's it, I suppose. You put it well.'

'It hurts a bit, though, Anthony, because I hadn't given you any reason to feel that way, had I?'

'I didn't need a reason. I found my own reasons. Now. . .well, it just feels good.'

He stood up and came across to her as she stood by the sink, still holding the wet teacups. Coaxing them out of fingers that suddenly felt weak and fumbling, he laid them down to dry and took her hands in his, not caring that they, too, were wet.

'Time for you to go to bed, Jennie.'

'Me? I thought I'd stay till——'

'I'm staying. I wouldn't sleep anyway.'

'Not your headache?' She looked searchingly up at him but couldn't see those tell-tale papery creases of tension around his eyes and mouth.

'No, that's completely gone now.' He cocked his head to one side for a second, thinking. 'Do you know, I wasn't even aware of it disappearing?'

'But perhaps you *do* need to sleep, or it will come back,' she insisted, wishing that she could lie with him somewhere and hold him until he fell into a dreamy slumber. His hands were still imprisoning hers in their warmth.

'I probably do,' he acknowledged, gently chafing her fingers. 'But I need to think, too, and as you said to me earlier today—yesterday, really, I suppose—nothing in medicine is ever routine. In spite of all good appearances, I'd like to keep a pretty close eye on Mrs Astwood and baby Michael tonight.'

'All right, then. I *am* tired,' she admitted, as she suddenly felt the full force of fatigue washing over her. It was Anthony's touch, making her weak.

'But before you go, Jennie. . .' he murmured, so low that she almost didn't catch the words.

And then he was kissing her, taking her lips with his mouth and releasing her hands to bring his up and cup her jawline so that he could raise it to meet the sensual onslaught of his touch. With a shuddering sigh, Jennie surrendered herself to everything she felt, and wrapped her arms around him—his lower back at first, where there was a faint, taut hollow, and then upwards to the full breadth of his chest and shoulders, chafing her palms against the fine cotton of his shirt and wishing that she could feel the warmth of his skin instead. . .

Their kiss went on and on, and with each passing moment Jennie knew that she was closer and closer to being lost, to giving herself to him completely.

'Jennie. . . Genevieve. . .'

This was his cabin and this was night-time, a Wednesday night, only three days now until she would arrive in New York harbour aboard the *Leeward* for the last time. It was almost a month since the night when the Astwoods' baby had been born—a month of passionately sensual discovery, long hours of talking and laughing together. . .and long silences in which

Jennie ached to tell Anthony everything she was thinking and feeling, fearing and hoping, but didn't dare.

He had never suggested that they sleep together, either with words or with the urgent demand of his body. Her own kisses were as hungry as his and somehow they both found a way to stop those kisses each time before they went too far. Like now. . .

It was dark in the cabin when they returned to it after a snatched two hours off for dinner ashore in a quiet St George's pub-restaurant where the menu was simple but appetising. As they had entered, she had reached for the light switch but he had whispered, 'Don't. . .' and moments later they were locked together.

How much time passed she didn't even try to guess, lost in the sensation of his hands on the most tender parts of her skin as he peeled aside the slim straps of her black crêpe dress so that it slid downwards to reveal the taut, creamy mounds of her breasts. Arching her back to meet his touch, she slid her own fingers beneath his shirt to play with the sculpted muscles of his back, and then they fell to the softness of the bed and clung to each other in the darkness. Each seemed to know that this was the moment for it to stop, if it was going to stop at all, and for Jennie, at least, it *had* to stop.

'I'm leaving in three days,' she said through lips that felt numbed and trembling.

'I know.'

And that was all. If she had been hoping for something more from him. . .*if*? Of course she had!. . .then it didn't come. Please tell me it won't be the end, she wanted to say. Tell me to wangle a last-minute extension to my contract, after all. Tell me you'll take a break soon and fly to England to see me. Tell me we'll *write*, at least!

But she was too frightened of his answer to speak the

words. Whatever he said, he would probably manage
to be very kind. . .

In the darkness, there was a distance between them
now. He was no longer touching her, and quickly she
adjusted her dress, knowing that she had to leave. He
didn't try to stop her, but stood and went to the light
switch by the door, flooding the room with a white
fluorescent brightness that seemed very harsh, coming
so suddenly.

'We're both off tomorrow until two,' he said. 'I
thought we could take a picnic brunch to have ashore.'

A casual suggestion, and she tried to make her own
voice as casual in return, although her feelings were
anything but. 'I'm not sure that's a good idea,
Anthony.'

'Why not?'

'Well, to begin with, I'm leaving on Saturday. . .'

'I know. Haven't we just said that?'

'I have things to do. Last-minute things.' And tonight
has been painful enough. I don't need tomorrow as
well. I've been crazy to keep seeing you, being with
you like this, over the past month. But I've been hoping
against hope. . .she added silently.

'Souvenirs to buy? I'll help you.'

'No, not souvenirs. I've got those. Laundry. Packing.
My flight to Edinburgh leaves at two on Saturday
afternoon, remember. That doesn't give me much time
if we're busy with on-call work over the next two days.'

For a moment, she thought he was going to argue,
then it looked as if he wasn't going to say anything at
all. His dark eyes were narrowed and he was watching
her face, where heat came and went with uncomfortable
suddenness.

'Couldn't you get some of it done tonight?' he said
finally.

'I'll try.' A vague promise. Easy to say tomorrow

morning that she hadn't got much done and still needed the time. She waited for his response. Would he guess her intention?

Evidently not. 'All right, then. I'll knock on your door at nine tomorrow and see how your suitcases are shaping up.'

'OK.'

'Our last day together, Jennie, before——'

'Yes. It would be nice. I'll try and pack tonight.' Very strained.

At last she was alone next door in her own cabin. It was only nine o'clock, but very deliberately she lay down on her bed and read a detective novel—not even a very good one—until she felt sleepy, making no attempt whatsoever to do any laundry or packing at all.

The next morning, Anthony was as good as his word, appearing promptly at nine. It had been a quiet night with no on-call work for either Tilly or the senior doctor, who had both been rostered on from nine until nine. Now, the Filipino nurse was in the staff mess eating breakfast and Jennie was standing nervously—and miserably—at the door of an immaculately tidy cabin.

Anthony noticed the state of perfection at once. 'No chaos? You must have finished, then.'

'No, not quite. I'm afraid I still need——'

'Not *quite*? Jennie, this isn't what a place looks like when someone is halfway through packing. Either you've finished or you haven't started at all! Why are you fobbing me off like this? Don't tell me I've misunderstood how——' He broke off and swore capably under his breath, then muttered almost incoherently, 'Damn it, in that case it's even more important that we get off this ship, talk, whatever it takes. . .'

Unceremoniously he wrenched open a wardrobe and saw dresses, blouses and jeans still hanging neatly on

their hangers and, at the bottom, two suitcases and a
plastic bag that was half-full of dirty laundry. With even
less ceremony, he dragged the suitcases out, opened
them up and flung them on the bed.

'Don't! What are you doing?'

'Isn't it obvious? I'm packing. It can be done very
quickly, you know, when a person has more important
things to do with their time!' He seized the bag of
laundry and squashed it into the bigger suitcase. 'There!
Your mother has a washing machine, I'm sure, and
probably a better one than the staff machines here on
board. Now, dresses. You want them lying flat, I
suppose, so——'

'*Stop* this!' His high-handed treatment of her belongings had roused her to a fury that drowned, for the
moment, everything else that she felt towards him.
Actually, it was a relief. 'How dare you do that? I've
told you I don't want——'

'But *why*, Jennie?' He was as angry as she was,
beseeching as well, and he rounded on her, dropping
last night's black cocktail dress in the middle of the
floor. '*Why*? This is our last day together, before——'

'Yes! Precisely! You keep saying that, drumming it
relentlessly into my head. Our last day together. Our
last day. Do you think I *want* a "last day" with you?
Haven't you noticed how I feel? You have, I know, and
I can't understand why you're being so cruel, so falsely
sentimental. You're as bad as Hector.'

'If you think what I'm doing today has *any* resem-
blance to Hector. . .!'

'Of course it does! He has a romantic "last day" with
a woman every week. He loves it. He doesn't stop to
think, even after the Melanie Nicholson episode, that
every now and then one of those women might actually
be hiding some real hurt under all that hair and make-
up he seems to go for. But to me that sort of thing

means nothing, and the only thing that is going to make my leaving you remotely bearable is if we just go on as usual and ——'

'Jennie, Jennie. . .' He came up to her, laying soft, stroking hands on her arms and running them up to her shoulders to caress her neck.

'Stop it! Don't!'

'Genevieve, please!'

'No!'

'Can't a man be allowed to plan a day of real romance? Not false sentiment. Not that! Romance. . . and love. I wanted to take you to some wonderful spot today, feed you all sorts of delicious things. . .and give you this.'

'Love? What. . .?'

He had reached into the pocket of a light windproof jacket, pulled out a small blue velvet box, and opened it up to show her a gold ring set with one diamond and, on either side of it, a row of three softly blue-green aquamarines.

'It doesn't have to be an engagement ring, if you want to choose that yourself. I'll give you as many rings as you want, Genevieve McDougall. But when I saw it, I thought of you and of us, Bermuda, the *Leeward*, the sea. A diamond for the late afternoon light shining on the salt spray that the ship's prow sends up into the wind, and aquamarines for the colour of the water where we first swam at Horseshoe Beach, and all the swims we've had there since.'

'Are you. . .asking me to marry you?'

'You've forced me to! Heaven knows. . .' he shook his head ruefully '. . . I wanted to wait until I got you alone in Ferry Point Park, but it began to seem as if I never would.'

'Oh, Anthony. . .'

Much later, when they *had* found a secluded spot in

Ferry Point Park, overlooking the water of Whale Bone Bay, she said to him, 'But you told me. . .you let me know in so many ways that you weren't going to do this; that life on the *Leeward* was not "real" for you, it was an interlude, and you'd never allow it to encroach upon your future.'

'I know. I did say it, and mean it, then. I was a fool, wasn't I? You were right about that when you hissed it at me that day in the Crystal Caves.'

'Weren't you angry, though, about that?'

'Of course I was, at first. I was barely civil to you for the rest of the week, if you remember.'

'I do, actually, yes!'

'But then I forgot about it. You seemed to trust my decisions about the future more than Stephen trusted them, and I came to value that so much. Came to value *you*. Came to want to talk to you about my addiction, and as soon as I did it all fell into place. I stayed up most of that night with the Astwoods thinking it all out and by morning I was sure. I'd come to need you, to love you and to know that I had to have you in my life. My whole life. The life I'll have. . .*we'll* have, when we go back. But I couldn't just blurt it all out then and there. We still needed time, don't you think? Until this morning. . .'

'When you threw all my clothes into those suitcases?' she teased.

'I thought you understood that.'

'Now I do.'

'How could you have thought that I'd kiss you so much and not mean anything by it?'

'I *should* have known. . . But it's a long wait,' she sighed. 'Nine months.'

'Jennie, love, I'm not going to renew my contract now.'

'But I thought you already——'

'The deadline for resigning is Saturday. I've already written the letter, taking back my offer to stay for another stint. They'll easily get someone else. Nine more months! Lord, do you think I could stand that? One month without you, until my resignation takes effect, is going to be bad enough!'

'The longest month of my life. . .'

'I've another letter, too, which I hope you'll take back to England for me and give personally to Stephen Greer,' he said, many minutes later.

'You mean. . .?'

'I'm going to take the research position. And we'll find a house somewhere outside London.'

'Perfect!'

'As close as it gets,' he whispered into her hair.

Before them, as they sat on a tartan picnic rug, waves feathered and ruffled on to a rocky shore, and beyond the white lace of the foam the sea shaded from aquamarine to turquoise and sapphire, to an indigo midnight-blue. In the balmy air, you would never guess that it was late October now.

Following a severely worded order from Anthony, Jennie sat back lazily and watched him as he began to unpack the late breakfast picnic he had brought in a basket. Coffee in a Thermos, fruit fresh in its peel, and several croissants and pastries, buttery and sweet.

'There's a lot more to tell you,' he said as he poured a strong, milky brew into her cup. 'I phoned my parents late last night. Couldn't sleep, actually, thinking about you. I told them I planned to come home and take up the position with Stephen.'

'They were pleased, I hope.' Jennie wasn't yet convinced that she was going to like these parents of his, although his brother sounded very nice. . .

'Very pleased. Although my mother's astonishment

that the man should still want me was a little unflattering.'

'Anthony, I'm going to have a bit of trouble with my temper in some areas of our marriage. . .'

'Ever heard the expression "grin and bear it"?' he teased. 'On the positive side, my father has decided to retire, and they're going to live in the south of France, which both of them will love. He would have given me his practice. Now he'll sell it.'

'Are you sure you don't want to take it over and——?'

'*Quite* sure! And the news from this side of the Atlantic: Hector is thinking of getting married!'

'*What*?'

'Oh, he hasn't actually met the girl yet. His sister will introduce them back in Colombia if he doesn't renew his contract in four months' time. Apparently she's a beauty, twenty-three, of quite good family, and anxious to settle down.'

'What more could a man want?' Jennie murmured, her blue eyes twinkling mischievously.

'Well, I can think of a few things that *I'd* want,' he drawled, setting their coffee-cups carefully out of the way before he pulled her down on to the picnic rug. 'For a start, she'd have to be you. . .'

And, by the time the kiss had ended, their coffee was quite cold.

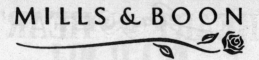

MILLS & BOON

LOVE ON CALL

The books for enjoyment this month are:

A MAN OF HONOUR Caroline Anderson
RUNNING AWAY Lilian Darcy
THE FRAGILE HEART Jean Evans
THE SENIOR PARTNER'S DAUGHTER Elizabeth Harrison

♥ ♥ ♥ ♥ ♥

Treats in store!

Watch next month for the following absorbing stories:

TROUBLED HEARTS Christine Adams
SUNLIGHT AND SHADOW Frances Crowne
PARTNERS IN PRIDE Drusilla Douglas
A TESTING TIME Meredith Webber

Available from W.H. Smith, John Menzies, Volume One, Forbuoys, Martins, Tesco, Asda, Safeway and other paperback stockists.

Also available from Mills & Boon Reader Service, Freepost, P.O. Box 236, Croydon, Surrey CR9 9EL.

Readers in South Africa - write to:
Book Services International Ltd, P.O. Box 41654, Craighall, Transvaal 2024.

HEART  HEART

Win a year's supply of Romances
ABSOLUTELY FREE?

Yes, you can win one whole year's supply of Mills & Boon Romances. It's easy! Find a path through the maze, starting at the top left square and finishing at the bottom right.

The symbols must follow the sequence above.

You can move up, down, left, right and diagonally.

START

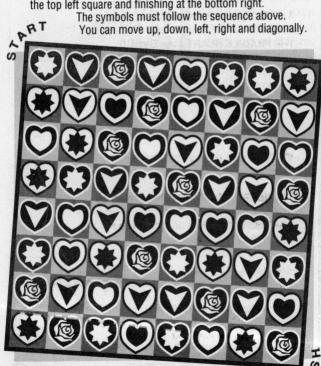

FINISH

Please turn over for entry details

HEART ⊕ HEART

SEND YOUR ENTRY NOW!

The first five correct entries picked out of the bag after the closing date will each win one year's supply of Mills & Boon Romances (six books every month for twelve months - worth over £85).
What could be easier?

Don't forget to enter your name and address in the space below then put this page in an envelope and post it today (you don't need a stamp).
Competition closes 31st November 1994.

HEART TO HEART Competition
FREEPOST
P.O. Box 236
Croydon
Surrey CR9 9EL

Are you a Reader Service subscriber?   Yes ☐   No ☑

Ms/Mrs/Miss/Mr   D. L Dyer _____ COMHH

Address 63 WOODWATER LANE,

HEAVITREE, EXETER,

DEVON,

Postcode EX2 5NQ

Signature   D L Dyer

One application per household. Offer valid only in U.K. and Eire. You may be mailed with offers from other reputable companies as a result of this application. Please tick box if you would prefer not to receive such offers. ☐